the **americas**

Mariposa's Song

Mariposa's Song

A Novel

Peter LaSalle

Texas Tech University Press

This book is typeset in Fairfield. The paper used in this book meets the minimum requirements of ANSI/NISO Z39.48-1992 (R1997). ∞

Designed by Kasey McBeath
Cover illustration by Irma Sizer

Library of Congress Cataloging-in-Publication Data
LaSalle, Peter.
    Mariposa's song : a novel / Peter LaSalle.
        p. cm. — (The Americas)
    ISBN 978-0-89672-743-4 (hardcover : alk. paper) —
ISBN 978-0-89672-781-6 (pbk. : alk. paper) —
ISBN 978-0-89672-775-5 (e-book)
    I. Title.
    PS3562.A75246M37 2012
    813'.54—dc23   2012033484

Printed in the United States of America
12 13 14 15 16 17 18 19 20 / 9 8 7 6 5 4 3 2 1

Texas Tech University Press
Box 41037 | Lubbock, Texas 79409-1037 USA
800.832.4042 | ttup@ttu.edu | www.ttupress.org

for those who are undocumented, in any place
and in any way

"Not only is it good policy, it's good politics."

—from a prominent state office holder in Texas,
on keeping tough on immigration

Some material from this novel, in different form, has previously appeared in the *New England Review* and *Witness Magazine,* and the author is grateful to the editors of these publications.

Mariposa's Song

. . . and Mariposa was working at the club, she didn't show the Anglo her scars at first, and at first she probably didn't notice him at the club, El Pájaro Verde on East Sixth Street there in East Austin that hot Saturday night, Mariposa didn't notice him even if he was an Anglo, because what did anybody notice at the so-called club, El Pájaro Verde, it was always a sort of dream, something Mariposa suspected was there but was never quite sure about, and sometimes for Mariposa it surely felt as if she wasn't there, as if the men weren't telling her how pretty she was, twenty-year-old Mariposa with her caramel skin and oversize hazel eyes, almost amber, her lustrous dark hair and maybe too skinny in her jeans and lime-green halter top, all of which, if nothing else,

made her look different than the other girls who worked
with her, mostly Mexican, but Mariposa wasn't Mexican, she was from Honduras, and it wasn't any dream,
she surely was now working in Club El Pájaro Verde on
East Sixth Street, East Sixth Street in that old Mexican
pocket of the city on the other side of the elevated interstate, East Sixth Street and the stubby cross streets with
tumbledown wooden cottages painted hopeful pastels,
faded blue and faded yellow and faded pink, junk cars
up on blocks in the weedy drives of crushed caliche,
worn red dirt yards with ceaselessly barking bony dogs,
clusters of thick-trunked old Washington palm trees
shedding piles of dead fronds, and *always* the smell of
the cooking everywhere, its pervasive corn-oil aroma,
in the neighborhoods around East Sixth, once the main
street, where now you might step outside the club to
the cracked sidewalk and see in the continuing autumn
heat even at nine at night the silhouetted bell tower of
Cristo Rey Church in the strong moonlight, you could
watch the men wearing ball caps or cheap straw Western *sombreros* walking, wandering from bar to bar, all
cautious, most illegal, *indocumentados*, the men maybe
half startled and thinking that they themselves were
dreaming there was such a thing as a Saturday night
and they could actually spend some of the green bills

worn as soft as flannel that they didn't dare put in any
bank, when at last they weren't muscle-aching and out
of breath, climbing up and down ladders, wrestling with
the screeching Skilsaw, lugging the sacks of ready-mix,
sometimes even scurrying like crazed mice to just flee as
fast as they could, anywhere, everywhere, as there came
the long, looping two-finger whistle from somebody
who had spotted *la migra* and *los agentes* in one of their
huge-tired government SUVs rumbling toward another
dusty work site still again, and after so few raids for so
long there now were many raids, Austin a supposed Safe
City or not, and for a while there were rumors of new
laws, but nobody working really cared or even knew
that much about those or any other new laws right now
in this year that somehow was already 2005, laws were
for the bosses, the people with money who were those
other than them, there was Club El Indio and Club Tío
Raúl's and Club El Pájaro Verde, which was where Mariposa worked, a B-girl in a place that amounted to little
more than a *cantina*, and, no, she didn't even notice the
Anglo at first, she had gotten to the club early, she had
listened to Mr. Álvarez talk to the girls, though maybe
she hadn't really listened, because for Mariposa there
was sometimes a song, and . . .

. . . and, before that, hurrying from where she lived with her aunt and going to the club that night, she wanted to make sure she was there a bit early, she had no watch, she had two white plastic bangle bracelets on each wrist, they clicked, Mariposa had no watch but she knew about time, how on any job it was good to be early, time was important, more important than it was back in Honduras, the minutes and all the hours that probably still slowly, sleepily ticked away on the big clock with its black roman numerals atop the whitewashed *alcaldía,* the old municipal edifice with its lumpy red tile roof there in the central square of her town deep in the undulating green mountains, time wasn't very important in her town, but it was here, and English was very important here, she had to speak English more, she knew, she had to forget the sweet Spanish that she was raised on, and there was a song when she was a child in Honduras, "La canción de la Paloma," though when her grandmother who raised her sang it to her the good-natured woman changed it, made it not just "La canción de la Mariposa" but "La canción de *Mariposa,*" her name meant butterfly, it became her song, and sometimes

Mariposa thought that her life had been like that, the
butterfly fluttering so far away, she had traveled through
Mexico, from Chiapas to Nuevo Laredo, and she had
been in Tennessee, but she didn't like to think that
much about Tennessee, no, not at all, and that night
when all the girls had first arrived the owner Mr. Álvarez
had spoken to the girls again, Mr. Álvarez was a short,
stocky guy of just thirty-five or so with thinning hair and
wearing a light blue *guayabera*, loose tails and white embroidery up and down the pleated front, also too much
gold body jewelry, somebody who you wouldn't think of
as a "Mister" or even a "Señor" if you saw him, if you
didn't know him, you would simply want to call him by
his name of Luis, but he made it clear as soon as he
hired any girl that he should be called "Mr. Álvarez,"
and if any of them occasionally slipped and addressed
him otherwise he would correct them, and when the
Mexican girls whispered together they laughed about it,
they joked that maybe next they were supposed to call
him "Don Luis," as if he was some minor nobility or at
least one of those swashbuckling young handsomes who
owned a sprawling horse-breeding *estancia* and who all
the ravishingly beautiful women were vying for in the
telenovelas, they laughed about how he seemed to have
carefully arranged the strands of his thinning hair

combed straight back, like perfect stripes, but the Mexican girls didn't laugh at him when he was around, and
when he called them together before the Saturday
crowd would arrive that night, he told all of them that
they probably would be very busy because of the heat,
he said people always came out to bars in the heat and
the girls would have to keep things moving, he told
them in Spanish, Inés nodded more than anybody else
because Inés was like that, sometimes playing up to Mr.
Álvarez, Inés didn't like Mariposa, Mariposa knew, she
didn't like her at all, and even as the girls stood there at
the bar and listened to Mr. Álvarez going on, Mariposa
could sense that Inés wanted to tell the other girls that
they wouldn't have to get this lecture if it wasn't for
Mariposa, yes, perky, too-cheery Mariposa, as far as Inés
was concerned, Mariposa who seemed intent on keeping things moving and just wanted to make the rest of
them look as if they weren't working hard enough, the
way Inés probably saw it, but Mariposa wanted to tell
Inés that she couldn't help it if she was busy, if the men
kept coming up to her, to dance, to order for her another one of those overpriced little squat red cans of Tecate
for ten dollars along with their own longneck bottle that
cost only three, a miniature Tecate that the girl hardly
even sipped, but that was the way it worked at Club El

Pájaro Verde for a B-girl, the men were buying company
for a while, they were far away from home themselves
without their families and they had loneliness that hurt,
you were convinced, as much as their muscles and very
bones from their long hours of work, loneliness that
showed sometimes frighteningly, and it could have been
that Mariposa was popular with the men because she
was different, Honduran, and Mariposa wasn't trying to
make anybody look bad or lazy or not working hard
enough, and until the smiling Anglo who told her his
name was Bill came in that night (she had no way of
knowing about who he really was), Mariposa until then
had never before shown anybody else in El Pájaro Verde
the scars, to be honest, and they were on the palms of
her hands lower down, a place where you never thought
that you could get scars, the skin supposedly thick
there, but Mariposa had gotten the burn scars, ripply
like satin, reddish, and though they didn't hurt like they
used to hurt, achingly, they had never gone away, proof,
if only to herself, that she had spent almost a year in
Nashville in Tennessee, her older brother was living
there with his wife and kids, he was all but legal and
forever hoping for a green card, he had a good job driving a delivery truck for a computer-supply chain store
called Completely Wired, he had worked his way up

from a job on the loading dock and then eventually was allowed to drive the brand-new red-and-white delivery van, he had most everything now, he had what they called a commercial-operator driver's license, he had his family with him, so when he made the long-distance call to their grandmother who had raised them in Honduras he said that it could all happen for Mariposa, too, or if it had happened for an *idiota* like him, he laughed, it surely could happen for her, and soon Mariposa was going up through Guatemala and then Mexico, and in Mexico the buses had video monitors that showed terrible movies, old, awful dubbed movies with Stephen Segal or Whoopi Goldberg that everybody on the buses almost tried to hide from as the tires sped along, and some of those on the buses wrapped themselves under jackets or sweaters still deeper so they wouldn't have to hear any of the loud dubbing in those awful movies, and then across the border, which had been easy enough for Mariposa, nearly comical and unbelievable it had been so easy, and for months she had told herself that she was willing to try almost anything to get into the U.S., though even while back at home she had already had nightmares about what she had seen broadcast on the Honduran national TV station in Tegucigalpa, the film footage somehow always taken at night and showing the shadowy figures climbing over high fences with razor wire in California or the shadowy figures stumbling half lost through some dark desertscape of saguaro cacti and the scattered litter of big gallon water jugs and who knows how many, yes, *shoes* lost along the way in the dreamlike sands in Arizona, all of it even worse than the simple dimness of the taped scenes, because in the badly lit films probably taken with some kind of special night camera the figures seemed to be beyond shadowy, they were ghostly, they seemed to be moving through a dull greenish landscape or a dull bluish landscape, netherworlds, nightmarish indeed, and everybody in her town knew the stories of the vicious *coyotes*, everybody knew the stories of those found suffocated, bodies bloated like so many chickens stinkingly roasted in the oven that was the back of a van or old panel truck, the doors still padlocked shut by the *coyote* who had quickly fled when he spotted the border patrol, a dozen dead, two dozen dead, everybody in her town knew and talked about those stories, they had been warned, but for Mariposa it hadn't been like that whatsoever, and in the cheap hotel room off the main square in Nuevo Laredo, paid for with the money her brother had sent, she did end up staying three days, she had to wait for Friday night, that was what her friend Lourdes had told her to

do, explaining it to her very carefully and very clearly,
Mariposa also had to get brave enough, she tried to con-
vince herself that as a child growing up she had always
been brave, and with her brother and her being without
their parents and raised by their *abuelita* she had
learned to be brave, she had to be brave now, and she
didn't wander far from the little hotel room with its
cracked yellow walls and a single bare bulb dangling
from a squiggly black cord, also a filthy toilet usually
overflowing, which she didn't even want to tell the
creepy guy at the nook for the check-in desk downstairs
about for fear of drawing attention to herself, she spent
a lot of time pushing aside the thin red curtains just a
bit to look outside and down to the park of the central
square where the city buses and *peseros* pulled up growl-
ingly, where in the empty dew-covered mornings it was
always the same ritual, the ragged men who had slept
the night somewhere in the park, amidst the frilly band-
stand and the green benches, the black statues of the
honored heroes of the República and the massive trees
with their trunks whitewashed lower down, one by one
the men would come out of the park to the payphone
on a pole right there across the street from Mariposa's
second-floor room in that place called the Hotel
Alameda, at dawn, and Mariposa would look down and

watch yet another one of them go up to the phone as if programmed to do so, run dirty fingers through the change slot of the phone in hopes of finding a few bronze centavos that were never there, walk away again as if wearily programmed to do so, and for a while Mariposa did get discouraged in Nuevo Laredo, a place that everybody knew you weren't supposed to spend too much time in, Nuevo Laredo was where the drug cartels were fighting for territory, they had lately taken to actually rocketing each other's houses in the *narcotraficante* war that was in full force now, and even when Mariposa was in Nuevo Laredo for those three days it was all continual sirens and confusion, a new police chief had been appointed to replace the old police chief and he was gunned down near the rickety *lucha libre* arena only blocks away from the Hotel Alameda there on Calle González and the central square, Mariposa saw live coverage of it in the little hotel lobby of green rubber tile where there was a big tropical fish tank beside the color TV, she sat alone on one of the chrome-legged chairs in the few rows of chairs set up as if in a classroom or little theater and saw on TV the corpse of the fat police chief, bald and mustached, in his blood-soaked uniform and video-taped from every angle while still slumped at the wheel of a car, his police SUV that seemed more just a splattering of deep pits of automatic-gunfire holes than what was left of the polished black sheet metal of the SUV itself, and in the course of the long days in Nuevo Laredo Mariposa thought often of what she woke up to in Nuevo Laredo, what she herself saw when she came into the world of supposed daylight after her own dreaming on the sagging bed that smelled of urine and cigarette smoke, to push the flimsy red drapes aside again and see the lost men one by one coming out of their own uneasy dreaming to wander up to the pay-phone and scoop fingers over that metal probably worn shiny with their perpetual clawing, hoping for forgotten change but for there to be nothing there, and Mariposa sensed that maybe she had come this far, all the way from her Honduras to Nuevo Laredo, to be so *close*, but for there to be, true, nothing here for her either, it was a mistake to have left home, yet Mariposa did what her friend named Lourdes back in her town beyond Teguci-galpa had told her to do, very clearly, Lourdes like a par-ent instructing, it was the best way, Lourdes assured her, or Lourdes said it was what Mariposa should at least try, so after three days in Nuevo Laredo Mariposa put on a clean blouse she had been saving from the clothes that she carried in the single handbag, not even a shoulder bag, she put on some makeup and lipstick, and wearing the fresh white blouse with her jeans, she checked out of the Hotel Alameda at eight o'clock that Friday evening, not arguing when the creepy guy at the desk told her that she would have to pay for another full day, she had remained there well after check-out time already, OK, she told him, she paid, and outside she noticed how, an ongoing drug war or not, Nuevo Laredo did find itself filled with gringo tourists on Friday night, just as Lourdes had said, they came in couples or in bunches from across the two bridges connecting to the Texas city of Laredo, they packed the restaurants that smelled of *cabrito* grilled over orange flames of huge barbecue pits, the charred carcasses displayed in the front windows and *cabrito* supposedly a Nuevo Laredo specialty, and along the main street the tourists moved in and out of the stark, open-front white *farmacias*, of which there were a lot in Nuevo Laredo, always a green first-aid cross glowing outside each *farmacia* and an attendant in a white lab coat standing behind the counter, surely ready to sell you everything that the touts who trudged around the city with fliers all day promised was available, pain killers and sleeping pills and especially, and always, Viagra, with the prescriptions issued right on the spot, and the tourists were very thick in the row of shops just before the older of the two international bridges, shops selling souvenirs and heat-warped post-cards on swivel racks, selling absurd mariachi *sombreros* and so much ceramic pottery and the Mexican throw rugs striped brightly like blankets, Mariposa bought a little rug with end fringe like string, she bought a terra cotta flower pot, glossily ceramic and showing a blue-and-yellow patterning of giant birds, and at eleven o'clock, as Lourdes had instructed her, she just tried to lose herself in the crowd walking along on the sidewalk, all those tourists and rowdy American college-age kids coming out of the bars drunk and themselves returning to their cars that they had left in Laredo on the Texas side, they wouldn't dare drive their cars over the bridge to Nuevo Laredo, especially with the reputation of the city lately, the crime there, and the whole idea of it was for Mariposa to look like a happy tourist, Lourdes had told her what to do, instructed her, and with the traffic that could build up then on the bridge and with the crowd of certainly happy tourists, the border officers got overwhelmed at that hour and could only pick out somebody here or there to pay real attention to, in all likelihood she would get waved though, and Mariposa had the rug under one arm and the big blue-and-yellow ceramic clay flower pot under the other, she kept close to a group that seemed to be college kids and she

smiled as wide and confidently as she could, her teeth
like bright shells, even acting a little put out by having
to juggle the things she was carrying and dig into the
pocket of her jeans to find the five pesos to put into the
slot to go through the turnstile on the Mexican side,
they charged you just to walk onto that long bridge span-
ning the wide, weedy flats of the trickling attempt at a
river, floodlights down there, and she playacted a bit
more when she got to the U.S. customs-and-immigration
concourse, all glass and gleaming stainless steel, jug-
gling some more the stuff she carried, nervous, not daring to look over to the hatless crew-cut muscular young
men in their dark blue uniforms with the somehow
frightening patch of the American flag on the shoulder,
she had to be brave, she had to get past the low metal
counters that they had there for you to slide your stuff
across for inspection, if you did, in fact, get singled out,
if you were waved over and not waved through, but
Mariposa *was* waved through, there was a crowd of people, noisy, Mariposa wasn't called aside and up to one of
the booths, they must have thought she was indeed a
tourist lugging back home what she had bought,
Lourdes had been right, and Mariposa was suddenly in
deserted and neatly groomed Laredo on the Texas side
as easily as that, she spent the night in the motel that

Lourdes had told her about right next to the Greyhound station, she left the rug and ceramic pot in the room, she hoped somebody would be happy to find them there, and while a bus for one of the Mexican lines operating out of Laredo and going north would cost half as much, Lourdes had also instructed her that a Greyhound was safer, the buses of Mexican companies got checked more often than Greyhounds beyond Laredo, yes, there might be a stop and inspection by *la migra* when the bus was pulled aside once it got outside of Laredo and into the barren Texas flatlands, but the Greyhound bus wasn't stopped, Lourdes's instructions were perfect, Mariposa stayed with her aunt in Austin for a week, and then she took another Greyhound bus up to Tennessee, and now in the club where she worked as a B-girl Mariposa thought that being back in Austin was, if nothing else, better than being in Tennessee, and it didn't work out there in Tennessee, even though her brother did get her a job at the store called Completely Wired, in the packing-and-shipping room, her English wasn't good enough, she didn't keep the job, so she went to work at the Burger King, and nobody cared about anybody's English very much, how good it was, at the Burger King, where she wore the baggy retro uniform they were having employees wear at the time,

brown and orange and bright yellow, some promotional
gimmick, where she got the painful scars, which probably wasn't even what finally made her leave Nashville
after less than a year there living with her brother and
his family, because when she was still back in Honduras
she had gone into the little library in her town to look at
a book with a map of the United States, she had seen
the "State of Tennessee," elongated and far away, but
not as far away as New York City and Chicago, which
everybody in Honduras knew were the really cold cities,
the ones where you never got warm in winter, where you
didn't want to go to if you didn't have to, but nobody
had ever told Mariposa that there would be snow in
Tennessee, but there *was* snow in Tennessee, it was so
cold, she was there in the winter, and even if she hadn't
been working at the Burger King, where let alone having
English, they didn't really care if you were anything
close to legal, and even if she hadn't had that terrible
job, Tennessee wasn't where she wanted to be, not at
all, the snow was white and quiet and very ghostly, so
frightening, Austin was better, warmer, no, she didn't
show the Anglo the scars at first, and before the Club El
Pájaro Verde got really crowded that night, Mariposa
made an effort to arrange things on the bar, Mr. Álvarez
liked to have the girls do that, to keep busy even before

the place was busy, and she didn't notice the Anglo right away, his name was Bill (she had no way at all of knowing about him, who he was), Mariposa didn't show him the scars at first, she really didn't, but maybe that was part of the dreaming of working there at the club, and …

. . . and she lived now in Austin, in her aunt's rented place on Chicón Street, sharing the cramped back room with two cousins still little kids, her aunt didn't like the fact that she worked in a club on East Sixth, but Mariposa promised her aunt she would be careful, she wouldn't get into any trouble, she told her aunt that she was just a B-girl, meaning bar girl, sort of a combination waitress and taxi dancer without the tickets, really, and the men only wanted to dance with her, talk with her, they only wanted company, and Mariposa now arranged the napkins in three piles at intervals along the bar so they would be there when the girls would come up to the bar with their round trays and have to reach for one of them, to wrap a brown bottle of Coors or Budweiser in the cocoon of a white paper nap-

kin, Mr. Álvarez had a policy on that, he said that a man
liked to see the napkin wrapped around a brown bottle,
to keep it cool, done right in front of him, always, it was
part of the service a man expected from a waitress, so
the other girls who worked as bartenders were only supposed to do it if somebody was drinking at the bar, otherwise it was always done by the girls who worked as
waitresses, the B-girls, even Mariposa had learned early
on that if you lifted a beer off the big round brown plastic tray and then set it down on the table in front of a
man, if you lifted a napkin off that tray and used both
hands to carefully wrap it well like that, cupping it to
get the white of the napkin smooth and almost part of
the bottle, molding it, just the bottle's longneck poking
out and the beer label not visible at all, then you sometimes could get a good tip even if a man wasn't buying
you one of the little red cans of Tecate for ten dollars,
which entitled him to dance with you, which entitled
him to have you sit with him for ten minutes or so, fif-
teen at the most, and talk and laugh, which was really
the way to make money, and at the bar Mariposa tightened the two ties at the front of the lime-green halter
top that she couldn't ever get quite right, the flaps that
started at her bare back and tapered, wrapping around
to the front where you were supposed to fasten them in

a looping bow, there below Mariposa's smallish breasts, she had on jeans with embroidery she had done herself along the back pockets, she had on the one pair of dressy sandals, beige leather, that she had brought in the handbag that she carried past the customs-and-immigration officers in Nuevo Laredo, that she had carried all the way from her town in Honduras, her eyes were light hazel, what some might call amber, the men were always speaking of her eyes, and now Fat Tommy the bouncer was at the open front door in his too-small security guard uniform, which did look ridiculous on him, he was about Mariposa's age and very big, with Fat Tommy over six feet tall, he was black, what *norteamericanos* called African American, but he spoke Spanish well, he had been raised in East Austin, Fat Tommy, and it wasn't only how the dark blue pants were too short and you could see the twin slices of his very white athletic socks between the pants and the polished black work shoes, but also the way that the dark blue short-sleeve shirt didn't even quite button across his roly-poly stomach lower down and showed the equally very white of his T-shirt underneath, he was standing there in the door with his long flashlight, a day-glo orange plastic thing, gripped casually in his hand as if it was a cop's nightstick, maybe, but quiet, gentle Fat Tommy would

certainly never hit anybody with a nightstick, Fat Tommy, in fact, seldom even used the flashlight to check an
ID, only occasionally shining the beam on the little lam-
inated card of a driver's license to inspect the age of
somebody coming into Club El Pájaro Verde, examining
it under that flashlight, Fat Tommy's big hands clumsy,
he would squint to read it and slowly mouth out the syllables of what he read, the date of birth, as if he was
just learning to read, nobody seemed to really care
about how old somebody was in a club in East Austin,
the age of the girls working there included, and when it
came to East Austin nobody even seemed to care about
the new city ordinance about no smoking in bars or any
restaurants, Fat Tommy was framed by the doorway,
looking out to the blue moonlit night, hot, where you
could indeed see more men passing this way and that
on the cracked sidewalk, in those baseball caps tugged
low on the brow, in those straw Western *sombreros*, Fat
Tommy stepped inside and looked around the club, the
bar itself and the half-dozen tables near the bar that
were white porcelain on top and with the Carta Blanca
logo, old and wobbly tables, worn in spots to the black
underneath the porcelain by who knows how many
hands nervously tapping on them, as if the dirty finger-
nails themselves of so many drinkers had dug through in

spots, there was a low cinderblock wall painted the emerald green of everything else in Club El Pájaro Verde and it separated the small bar section from the dance floor, which was just a patch of scuffed black linoleum and at the corner of it the little raised platform for the disc jockey Espíritu who stood up there as if on an observation deck, wearing headphones that made him look like a Mars-man, with all his turntable gear and complicated panel of glowing controls sandwiched between the massive black speakers that you could almost see pulsate, the fabric flexing in and out, the sound enough to resonate and echo in your rib cage once the night got going, as the music became too loud and the smoke became too thick, the smoke would swirlingly cloud like yellow marble in the course of a busy night, you could jump into the coolest and very deepest ocean and your clothes would still have that smell, a smell that Mariposa sometimes thought she would never get rid of, not only in her clothes but in herself, the light was rigged up reddish in the dance section, on the walls everywhere there were big posters supplied by the beer companies, they showed buxom girls, sultry-eyed and always with the same abstract and sexily serious gaze, wearing bikinis and cowboy hats, maybe about to sip a beer with very pouty lips, other posters showed handsome soccer

stars from the Mexican teams in the thick of wild play,
Cruz Azul and also C.A., Club América, and especially
the revered Chivas, the ball booted, the players' inevitably long hair making the whole crowd of them, on both
teams and in any match, look like rock stars who had
somehow gotten dispatched to the wrong event on all
that greener-than-green of the stadium grass, Fat Tommy in the doorway stood there, slowly looked around
the club that was starting fill some with more men at
the tables, he obviously saw Mariposa carefully arranging the napkins, fluffed, she had the three stacks spaced
at intervals along the length of the bar that was only a
dozen feet or so long, and Fat Tommy nodded, Mariposa
smiled, she liked Fat Tommy, Fat Tommy didn't even
mind his nickname, everybody called him that, she had
talked to Fat Tommy that one day when she had gone to
the laundromat on Chicón to do the wash for her aunt,
she had found Fat Tommy sitting on one of the scoop
chairs in a row there in front of the thumping yellow
washers and dryers waiting for his own clothes, he had a
school textbook on his lap, leaning over it, and Fat Tommy was taking courses at the community college, ACC,
Mariposa knew, and now Mariposa still didn't have that
halter top right, the two ends of the flaps weren't tied in
a bow quite right, and, to be honest, she herself thought

that the top was stupid, she had bought it at the outdoor
marketplace set up in the parking lot on Pleasant Valley
where the clothes were new, racks of dresses and shirts
and jeans displayed under little tents, bins of socks and
shoes and sandals, and on Saturday and Sunday that
marketplace became the whole world of the *indocumentados* in Austin, you could shop for everything there, you
could eat there, you could have *tacos* or *menudo* or even
buñuelos fried in loudly bubbling deep fat there, topped
with crunchy sugar, it was just about the only place her
aunt herself shopped, Mariposa taking the big city bus
there with her aunt on Saturday morning when her aunt
was off at last from the long hours at the Pepsi bottling
plant where she worked, but Mariposa knew the danger
of that marketplace on Pleasant Valley Road, a winding
wide boulevard, everything was only for *indocumentados*,
for all it mattered you weren't even in America on Pleasant Valley, both at the marketplace and beside it at the
seventies-style four-plex movie theater with its glass
front and once-modern fancy chandeliers there that had
been converted into a makeshift two-floor mall of sorts
for *indocumentados*, most of them Mexican, admittedly,
the outdoor marketplace was set up on weekends in
what had been the theater's big parking lot, and in that
adjoining attempt at a mall of sorts housed in the former

theater was a food court restaurant for *mariscos* where
the men came on Sundays, always in their best clothes,
to buy the giant shrimp cocktails that probably cost a
couple of hours' worth of labor on their wearying construction jobs, because now in 2005 the building business overall was booming and there were plenty of such
jobs, jobs where the Anglo bosses shouted at them,
called them wetbacks and stupid donkeys, and the men
slowly forked the big pink *camarones* from the heavy
glass cups, long-stemmed and that probably held a gallon, or so it seemed, the shrimp thick in that peppery
gunk of red sauce, they slowly ate as if this was proof
that they were enjoying themselves, this was the mark
of being in Texas where you could eat a giant overpriced
Veracruz shrimp cocktail the size of a meal in itself with
a long fork and silently stare ahead at nothing along
with the other men on Sunday, as if the eating, too, was
work you had to do, and there was a Mexican hair-
styling "Salon" that was really just a big barber shop, the
girls with snipping scissors and buzzing clippers cutting
the hair of mostly men, there was a Mexican Western-
wear shop and a Mexican convenience store with
shelves of only Mexican canned goods, and there was,
maybe busiest, the little nook for money transactions,
not just a *cambio* where whatever Mexican peso bills

that you might have left in your pockets from home, their once bright poster-paint colors now a uniform dull brown on the worn-thin slabs, they could be changed almost through some uncannily deft sleight-of-hand trick into real green-and-gray American dollars, so crisp, so new, but, more importantly, in that nook there was the reverse of all that, the wire service to send money back home, where you asked for one of the bright yellow forms, where you filled it in with a pen, so carefully, all the boxes, and where you equally carefully counted out the American cash from your palm as others in line waited to do the same behind you, and she sometimes thought that maybe those money wires were the real butterflies, not the flying sort with her name of the butterfly, *mariposa,* and especially on a hot, hot night like this it would be easy to envision the hundreds and hundreds, no, surely thousands and thousands, of the yellow wire-order forms flapping in the blue night sky there in the moonlight and going south, even if it was all done electronically now and even if they probably had you fill out the yellow forms printed in such dark and important black ink only because the forms looked like what the old wire-order telegrams were supposed to look like, it was easy to picture them swarming onward, over all the moonlit jagged mountains and all the moonlit flats of cactus-shadowed deserts and all the very moonlit, very beautiful beast-crying jungles, even, of her faraway Honduras itself, flying, fluttering, beating on exactly like the swarms of real butterflies that you did read about migrating in clouds over so much geography, over continents, and in the converted movie theater that must have once been considered classy in the seventies and also in the noisy marketplace beside it that, true, could have been a happily ramshackle street *mercado* in Saltillo or Oaxaca or Monterrey, there where Mariposa had bought the lime-green halter top, yes, in all of it on Pleasant Valley the problem was that you spoke only Spanish there, she needed to learn English better, that had been the problem in Tennessee, that was why she was told not to come back after her second paycheck while working in the shipping room at the Completely Wired store, a paycheck for which all the tax and other deductions had been officially taken out using the long, hyphenated social security number that her brother had just come up with for her to use, somebody else's, he had shown her how to do that, he had explained to her that Completely Wired and also the U.S. Government didn't care whose social security number it was as long as they had some sort of a social security number, that was the way it worked, that was what her brother called the "game" of it all, not much different even with the recent supposed crack-downs, and the manager at the store had told her outright that she needed better English, but you didn't learn better English by just limiting your whole world to that converted movie theater and the marketplace in the parking lot beside it on Pleasant Valley, you had to deal with Anglos to learn the language, her brother told her, that was the secret to his unquestionable success, but it wasn't easy, improving your English, putting together the syllables that became the words that became the sentences, a language like English that sometimes, for everybody else, did seem so easy and so natural and something as taken for granted as morning sunshine or softly falling lavender summer rain, especially when you heard the words effortlessly and laughingly spoken on the comedy shows on TV that she watched with her aunt's two kids, her cousins, and Mariposa was responsible for taking care of them after they got out of school and before their mother, Mariposa's Tía Gloria, came back from her own day at the Pepsi bottling plant where she usually worked overtime, English was somehow almost *magically* easy for the kids, eight and nine, they spoke English near fluently, though her aunt who was raising the kids on her own without her long-gone husband had next to no English,

and it was the same when Mariposa in the afternoon
sometimes took another huge, freezingly air-conditioned
city bus down to the Dove Springs neighborhood, somewhere in between the interstate and the city's airport,
Mariposa wasn't sure exactly where, she just got on the
bus and knew at what corner to eventually get off, by
the Fuelman gas station and its mustard-yellow convenience store blanketed with loud graffiti, the windows
prison-barred, Mariposa bringing the kids with her to
look after them and also, there in Dove Springs, look
after the three kids of her aunt's friend Teresa who
worked with her aunt at the Pepsi bottling plant, Mexican and from Chihuahua, and Teresa's husband had a
job as a house painter, her three kids were all under ten,
and Dove Springs was even more Mexican than the
converted theater and marketplace on winding Pleasant
Valley Road, Mariposa would sit with all the kids she
was taking care of, they would be there in the small
front living room of Teresa's duplex apartment watching
the giant TV that Teresa's husband the painter was very
proud of, he was paying for it with credit at Best Buy,
there was the cheap furniture and the cheap wallboard
of the place and the cheap gold frames holding color
photographs of the kids bought from the school photog-
rapher and set up almost like an altar between two

cheap candles in glass holders for devotion to the Sacred Heart, olive-skinned, dark-eyed Jesus in his red robe pulled open to reveal an exposed heart that was thorn-tangled and aflame, stabbed with a cross on top, it was what was always depicted on the glass holders there, Jesus with arms out and lifting upward his punctured hands to invite the world into his comfort, the perpetual solace of his loving embrace, yes, the surroundings there might have been predictable and shabby, cheap, but the big-screen TV was, in fact, top-of-the-line, a Sony, and the kids would laugh and horse around as they pretended to watch the late-afternoon reruns of a show called *Everybody Loves Raymond* that wasn't funny and another show called *Will & Grace* that wasn't at all funny, and even when she understood some of the English those terrible shows weren't funny, but the kids all laughed, maybe more out of excitement than anything else, Mariposa sometimes thought, the hissing, machine-gun rat-a-tat-tat of the laugh tracks on the shows making the children dizzily giddy, making them think they were supposed to laugh, horsing around, excited, squealing, they would speak English to each other but with Mariposa they spoke only Spanish, so she wouldn't learn or improve her English in a place like Dove Springs either, and what was funny, what Mariposa would laugh to herself about and what was something funnier than all those stupid TV reruns with the loud laugh tracks, was the way that three other people who also lived in Teresa's two-bedroom apartment in Dove Springs would come and go, three men of varying ages who were also from Chihuahua and who seemed to have different jobs that took them to work at different times of the day, weary, baggy-eyed, dirty from labor, they would trudge in and trudge out of a tiny cubicle of a single room off the front room, probably taking turns with the two beds there that were really just mattresses on the floor, they wouldn't say much more than "Buenas tardes" to Mariposa, nodding, the flimsy white door opening and shutting, so that while they tried to be gentle with it, it still shook the walls of such flimsy sheetrock in the apartment, in a way the whole thing was sad but in a way it was, yes, what could be really funny for Mariposa, like something on Spanish-language TV, something that you might get in the comedy skits on a show like *Sábado Gigante* that everybody would watch back in Honduras on Saturday, everybody in every Latin American country watched *Sábado Gigante* if at home on Saturday night, Mariposa suspected, sometimes Mariposa thought that she wouldn't have been surprised if a thousand weary men came and went through that back bedroom door, like one of those tricks of packing clowns into a small Volkswagen car, it could have all been on *Sábado Gigante,* but you surely didn't improve your English by watching Spanish TV, either Univisión *or* Azteca América, and above all, she realized, you didn't improve your English by working as a B-girl in Club El Pájaro Verde, the place was filling up now, the men were arriving in bunches at Club El Pájaro Verde, Mariposa patted the front flaps of the lime-green top to try to get them to lay right, she thought about retying the entire contraption of it in a bow still again but she decided that she probably could never get the thing to sit right on her skinny torso, she was bra-less, because with a top like this you really couldn't wear a bra, though she now maybe wished that she had on her lacy black best one for more coverage, and when she had first worn the top with jeans and sandals on Tuesday night Mr. Álvarez had noticed that it was new, he had looked at her from the top of her thick, lustrous black hair, brushed back and falling onto her shoulders, to her feet in the dressy beige sandals and her stubby toenails painted red, it was the first time she had worn something like that to work at the club, what left her all but completely bare in back, so you could see the slightness of her shoulder blades and the delicately knotted rope

of her backbone, so you could see her tiny waist and the
small of her back above the curves of her behind in the
jeans with squiggly embroidery on the back pockets, Mr.
Álvarez said she looked good, he also said, making a
joke, that he never thought he would have a girl working
for him without a tattoo, he said that was good, he said
it was a *milagro*, in fact, to have a girl working for him
without some kind of tattoo somewhere, he said Mariposa should wear that top on weekends when there was
better business than on a Tuesday, so she wore it this
Saturday night, and always at the club, whenever she
did go out to the dance floor under that red light that
was hooked up so it flashed to a song's beat, whenever
she headed there to dance with the men who bought
her miniature Tecates for ten dollars, drinks that she
only sipped lightly once or twice, never really finished,
she always tried to keep smiling, she tried not to recoil
from how, before long, a man's hands wouldn't be just in
the usual dance stance, one hand in hers, the other below her shoulders, but soon both his arms out, the
hands looping together behind her neck as she shuffled
back and forth for a bouncy *norteño* song, all wheezing
accordion and rattling snare drums, the beat of it sounding from the huge speakers, and then the hands inevitably were on Mariposa's bare waist if she had worn a

short top, Mariposa's smooth skin, the man's rough hands like tree bark sometimes, like pebbly cement sometimes, there right above the Western-style belt on her jeans, a belt that she had had since she was back home in Honduras and that maybe was the kind of belt nobody wore anymore, but she liked it, it reminded her of Honduras, a boyfriend who did tooled leather-work had made it for her when she was still studying in school, the technical school there in her town, it was tan leather with a simple chrome buckle in front and on the back it had spelled out in frilly letters that were hand-painted a pretty turquoise and yellow her name "Mariposa" along with tiny white butterflies and flowers on either side of that, and the hands of a man dancing with her might slip down below the belt, might cup the roundness of her behind so trim and neat in those jeans, the fingers moving, which was OK, she was used to that, and Mr. Álvarez even instructed new girls about how men expected that on a dance, and while you could feel the fingers there holding you like a basket, even kneading, it was different when the heavy hands moved up again, past the tooled leather belt, maybe fingering the ridge of the blue jeans there, and then they would inevitably be on her bare waist, a hand on either side, Mariposa so small-waisted that a man's hands could

seemingly touch fingers and thumbs clasping her like
that, and the hands were very hard and rough, yes, like
tree bark sometimes, like pebbly cement sometimes,
almost scraping the smoothness of Mariposa there, but
the men were usually polite, they wanted to dance a little, they wanted to talk a little, they wanted what Mariposa knew was some human contact, to simply touch
another person, even if she couldn't have phrased it exactly like that herself, and though other things might go
on with some of the girls, though other things *did* go on
with some of the girls in the gravelly back parking lot
sometimes, out under the trees and by the dented alu-
minum trailer stand that sold the charcoal-smelling *faji-*
tas and the lurid green or lurid orange or lurid cherry-
red bottled Mexican soft drinks, too sugary, none of that
was Mariposa's concern, and a girl going with a man to
his parked car or a pickup truck, Mr. Álvarez had made
it clear, that was entirely the girl's own concern, and it
wasn't just drugs or, more so, the pot-smoking that went
on out there, because a lot of the girls did smoke pot,
there surely were the *other* things, but if a man suggested anything while dancing or did anything there in the
club itself that the girl didn't like, was uncomfortable
with, the girl was supposed to call for Fat Tommy, Fat
Tommy with his droopy bloodshot eyes and low, slow

voice would explain to the man that such behavior wasn't allowed, but Mariposa had had no problems with the men, and Mariposa tried to smile as all those rough hands moved up and down, and standing by the bar now Mariposa looked around the place herself (the man called Bill, this Anglo who she hadn't met yet, must have been in the nearby El Azteca Restaurant then, if she was to believe the story he later told her, he was from out of town, staying in a motel on I-35, he would tell her that he had come over to this side of Austin to have a meal of good Mexican food and see some of the neighborhood), and then Mariposa watched as Inés, who was a bit pudgy the way a lot of the men liked a girl to be pudgy, Inés got up from the table where she sat with some of the other Mexican girls and took the order at a table of two men in ball caps, top-heavy Inés wore an elasticized scarlet tube top that was no more than a frilled band around her chest, it emphasized her top-heaviness and showed so much of, well, that bare, displayed top-heaviness, there was no other way to describe it, she had black hair cut shorter in back for a bob and with a wing that flopped on her forehead in single piece and over her eye on one side, she had a small rhinestone stud in the side of her button nose that perhaps matched the larger rhinestone stud in the dent of

her navel, she obviously used a lot of Vaseline on her
eyelashes to make them look longer, or to make them
shine, her eyes were as black as her hair, and what Inés
did next was something she didn't have to do, but she
did it anyway, it wasn't any mistake, and maybe she had
been watching Mariposa arrange the napkins in the
three carefully placed piles along the bar, keeping busy
before the men arrived, maybe Inés had been laughing
about it with the other girls, especially Carmen who
sometimes could seem like Inés's sidekick, or lieuten-
ant, the two of them sitting with the other Mexican girls
at one of the white-topped Carta Blanca tables, and the
girl bartending put the two beers on the brown plastic
tray for Inés to serve, and standing next to Mariposa,
Inés, scented with the spicily sweet patchouli oil that
she used a lot of, she reached over to the napkin pile
with what she pretended, certainly, was just a quick
grab of her hand, and somehow in the course of picking
up a couple of the napkins to take with the beers to the
men, to wrap around their Budweisers, Inés somehow
just brushed aside the entire pile so that the napkins all
scattered on the bar top like strewn playing cards, some
of them even fluttering to the floor, and then reaching
for her tray Inés managed in the sweep to destroy the
better part of one of the other two piles Mariposa had

constructed, too, Inés making it all look like an accident, smiling so that you could see the dimples in her plump face, so that the glistening of the Vaselined eyelashes was even more obvious up close like that, she did have naturally long lashes, they were doll-like, she knew it, she probably didn't even need any mascara or Vaseline, then Inés going off to serve the beers and her very full behind pendulumming in her white jeans pegged at the bottom, her clear plastic high heels, and not getting angry, saying nothing to Inés, Mariposa then picked up a few of the napkins from the floor, beside the bar stool, Mariposa told herself that the whole trick was not to get angry about it, to assure herself *again* that working here was only temporary, and she didn't want to get into any trouble at the club, as she had told her Tía Gloria she wouldn't, and her Tía Gloria had been right, she *shouldn't* be working here, and all she could do now was to assure herself that she, Mariposa, would be away from the smoke of the place and the deafening music of the place once she could get something better (the Anglo named Bill must have finished the meal and been driving along East Sixth Street and looking at the nightclubs right about then, he must have been moving along slowly in his rental car with Arizona plates and glancing out the window open in the heat to see the cluster of them within a few blocks, Club El Indio and Club Tío

Raúl's, also Club Las Estrellas, small, and even Bar Tex-

as, one of the oldest clubs and still containing the long

mahogany bar proper in what had once been the scruffy

Hotel Texas with its redbrick facade and a tin awning on

posts for a portico stretching the entire length of the

building, a scene right out of some B-Western, and he

must have told himself, "That one looks authentic, all

right," then he must have seen the lit sign on another

building, an old buff stone place, two-storey, with its

blocked-off windows in front covered with plywood

painted gray, that green neon sign jutting out directly

above the door and saying in luminous tube-formed let-

tering CLUB EL PÁJARO VERDE, he must have seen the

open door and the young black guy there bulky enough

to be a football team's starting center and wearing a too-

small security guard uniform, just dreamily staring out

to the night, and this Anglo, who would tell her his

name was Bill, maybe said to himself, "This one looks

really good," nodding), Mariposa picked up more of the

napkins from the floor and threw them into the trash

bin in back next to the bathrooms that emanated the

pungency of strong disinfectant, and, as said, and to re-

peat what was explained earlier, she didn't show the An-

glo the scars at first, and . . .

. . . and for a while she brought beers to the different tables, Mariposa not thinking of much of anything, which was the way the dream of El Pájaro Verde could be sometimes, but Mariposa thinking of everything, La canción de Mariposa, and while Mr. Álvarez had thought the place would be packed on such a hot night, while he had taken the time to gather all the girls together earlier to give them the talk about getting ready for a lot of business, and while at about nine it actually had started filling up fast with more men arriving, by now, a half hour later, it seemed to have slowed down some, there seemed to be empty stools again along the bar, Mariposa arranged them, pushing them back closer to the bar after men would leave, she kept busy, then Mariposa seemed to be just standing there at the bar, more or less waiting, Inés sat and talked with the other girls at their table, one of them would now and then hear her cell phone ring and that would make her immediately pop up as if it was the most important thing in the world, as if it was a call saying that a producer wanted her to star in a major Hollywood movie, or as if

on the other end of the line was somebody breathlessly
telling her that she had won a million dollars in a lottery,
better than starring in a movie, you wouldn't have to
work at all, and the girl would go outside in a rush to
talk into the phone on the sidewalk, away from the music, and Inés kept her little silver cell phone poked into
that scarlet tube top, slightly off to one side of the split
of her sizable, half-exposed breasts, the tube top somehow frilled in the way it was pleated, elasticized, looking
like crumpled crepe paper and so low you wondered if it
was covering the buds at the tips of the fleshy chest that
Inés was without question very proud of, you would
look twice to check if it was, in fact, covering them, and
having the cell phone tucked there was maybe a better
trick than just wearing a rhinestone in your nose to emphasize that it was a cute button nose, as Inés did, and
it was better than just wearing a rhinestone in the lop-
sided knot of your navel to emphasize the miles of bare
brown flesh in between the crisp white Wrangler jeans,
pegged that way at the bottom, and the scarlet band of
the tube top, and, oh, how pudgy, top-heavy Inés would
make a big, dimpled, fully smiling show out of taking
her time before reaching for the cell phone on her chest
when it sounded its music, looking down at it with the
big eyelashes lowered, letting the tune play a few times

before she did reach for it, so anybody, everybody, would also look, see where the ringtone was coming from, Mariposa had seen Inés more than once do exactly that when with a man at a table, and sometimes Mariposa could almost laugh to think that maybe Inés and all the girls who had worked there for a while knew that there was some calculated joke to it, those other girls so unlike a new girl like Mariposa, the girls who usually had little to do with a new girl like her, so far, anyway, even after a month, and Inés probably had it all planned out and maybe she set the phone to ring every few minutes, you could probably do that with a cell phone, Mariposa didn't know much about cell phones and she didn't have one herself, she could have been the only girl who didn't have one, she didn't have the money for a cell phone yet, but she would save for one, though sometimes she thought that she really didn't know anybody who might call her except her aunt, so why did she need a cell phone, and when Inés went off to the dance floor with some man who led her out there, slowly, seriously, by the hand, when she next moved to sit at a table with him after the dance so he could buy her a ten-dollar Tecate, she would have the cell phone set, Mariposa imagined, so it would begin its melody once more, Inés letting it go on, letting the man of the sort most of the

men were, who did look so lost, so dazed by their hard
lives, stare at it ringing between her breasts, before she
plucked it and held it up to her ear, the little lumines-
cent greenish window of it glowing on her plump, dimpled cheek, showing the sparkle of the rhinestone on
her nose, but that was crazy, Mariposa thought, Inés
surely didn't do that, set the phone to ring to draw attention to her body, but it was funny to think that maybe she did do that, and Inés was now sitting at that usual Carta Blanca table off to the side of the bar with the
other girls, not all the girls, of course, just her group,
and on a Saturday like this there might be a dozen B-
girls working at El Pájaro Verde, including the older,
definitely chunky trio who possibly had been there forever, since they had been young, leathery skin now and
thick thighs and sadly heavy makeup, who didn't even
go out to the dance floor that much but just talked with
the younger men, sometimes one of these women would
go over to sit with one of the younger men at a table
alone, mothering the man who was very far away from
home, they did that sometimes, and to Mariposa the
trio of older women could seem like fortune tellers who
knew things about the men that they themselves, the
men, didn't know, would never have a chance of knowing, and still standing at the bar, now knotting the green

bow one more time to try to *finally* get it right, Mariposa
wondered if Ignacio would show this night, he had
come most every Saturday night during the month or so
she had been working there, handsome Ignacio and his
compadres, Ignacio tall and wearing his very best Western gear, the black felt Western hat, not a straw one, the
black Western shirt very neat, the black Western jeans
very neat, he had a fine silver belt buckle, the size of a
hubcap, it seemed, Ignacio was from Durango, he
would arrive with his four or five friends, he would buy
beers for his friends, Ignacio always polite, and Ignacio
had told her, not in any way bragging, that he was the
foreman for their crew at the site where they worked
construction, as his friends all confirmed it, they
seemed more proud of that fact than he was, his *compa-*
dres nodding, he was the important man among them,
yes, his friends all energetically assured her of his posi-
tion, though gentle, very handsome Ignacio, young, tried
to dismiss their compliments, change the subject, and
he had been promoted just the month before, his
friends more energetically assured her, and now Ignacio
had the best job of any of them at that construction site,
where they worked on what they explained to her was a
new condominium complex, downtown and not too far
from wide Congress Avenue, she learned all of that the

first time she had sat with them, and Ignacio told her
stories about his friends, quietly, because Ignacio could
tell a story quietly, smiling all the while, and he talked
about his own favorite *fútbol* team, Chivas in Guadalajara, the best of the best, and while most of his friends
agreed with him on that opinion, one of them, a small
guy, kept saying "Viva los Tiburones Rojos!," the Red
Sharks team, he was from Veracruz, he made a gesture
with his thumbs like horns put on top of his head of
curly ringlets to make fun of Chivas, the Goats, everybody laughed, handsome Ignacio and his friends were
nice, but Ignacio wasn't there yet, maybe he wouldn't
come with his *compadres* even if he had been there every other Saturday night, and sometimes Mariposa wondered if that was what made Inés and Carmen act the
way they did with her, if it was that she, Mariposa, had
proved popular right from that first night, even Mr. Álvarez seemed to recognize that, the men told her how
pretty she was, her smile, especially her hazel eyes almost a true amber, but she wouldn't let herself think too
much about it, and while Inés sat with her friends and
while the trio of older *mujeres* with all their eyeliner and
all their smeared-on lipstick went from table to table, *las
tres mujeres*, mothering, there were the other girls who
sometimes did seem as lost as Mariposa, some of them

who were even younger than Mariposa, and a few of them tonight did what they often did, sat around the video poker game at the bar and took turns reaching out to touch this card or that on the screen of the beeping contraption set on the bar top, none of them really understanding the game called poker but having their fun with it, nevertheless, fascinated with it the way kids might be fascinated with a glittering toy, *indocumentadas*, there was Concha and there was María and there was Fortunata and there was the one they just called Pinky, and across the low green cinderblock wall that divided the dim Club El Pájaro Verde in two, the red light flashed to the music, the disc jockey Espíritu wearing the big Mars-man headphones, Mariposa thinking of nothing, but Mariposa thinking of everything (*was there moonlight in her town in Honduras even now, and did the white alcaldía in the square amidst the neat palm trees still show its clock on top, a clock with big black roman numerals and ornate black hands trying to tell the time to anybody if he or she were willing to listen, trying to whisper it with the chiming of the hour, the long, lingering, but always so soft, metal notes that hung in the sweet and very fragrant air of her town in Honduras? was there the maybe admitted absolute futility of all those fluttering money telegrams, yellow and black from Western Union, still beating their way like butterflies southward over the mountains and deserts and jungles in the moonlight, going there but never getting there, because did anything really ever go anywhere, get anywhere at all, well, did it?*), and the DJ Espíritu would mix the music up, he would play a *norteño* song where the tuba might really hit you, not just an oomph that you could feel in your rib cage through the big speakers but more like somebody softly but solidly belly-punching you, it was strong and power-ful even amidst the accordion and drums, and then he would play a Mexican *cumbia* song with its hollow clip-clop beat like a horse lazily loping along, that beat in it-self seeming all there was once it got going, pounding you some, too, again making you forget the accordion and drums, because there were accordions and drums on all the songs, *cumbia* and *norteño* and even blaring *banda*, and sometimes to really mix it up he would play something totally different that would get what seemed like the entire place mouthing the lyrics everybody knew so well, usually an old *mariachi* number with its trumpets, violins, and melodic guitars and sung by Vi-cente Fernández, the guy with the thin, trimmed mus-tache, wearing the wide-brimmed *sombrero* and the fan-cy *charro* outfits of embroidery and silver inlay that he wore no matter what the setting was in one of the who

knows how many films he made, so if he was out at a
beautiful ranch in the countryside, he wore the outfit
and sang some songs, and if he was in modern, traffic-
clogged downtown Mexico City he did the same, in
those films that were really old and where the color
wasn't quite the true color, faded with age, more like it
was all a watercolor painting left out in the rain, the
sound off-key and distorted, movies that constantly re-
ran on TV even in Honduras when Mariposa had been
growing up, and when Espíritu put on one of those old
songs, all painfully slow, all unabashedly romantic, the
heartbroken pining-away to make for the sort of love
ballads where the many violins seemed to be hopelessly
and eternally sad themselves, weeping together, yes,
when one of those songs played, there was no shortage
in Club El Pájaro Verde of *ranchera* yelps, the extended,
cascading squeals, somehow sad, too, even if somebody
had once told Mariposa that it was originally the revered
battle cry of the *guerra de la indepencia* in Mexico, so it
was something very patriotic for Mexicans, the *grito*, but
Mariposa wasn't Mexican, she was Honduran, she was
different than the other girls, and still standing at the
bar she did what she usually did, she didn't want to just
stand there if there wasn't a table to serve, she could
only rearrange and straighten out so many times the old

stools with rusted chrome legs and cushioned tops of
glossily lumpy plastic that was supposed to look like red
mother-of-pearl, she didn't want to think about the napkins, what Inés had done just to show her that she,
Inés, *could* do it, and Mariposa could only check that
green bow again on her halter top so many times, and at
the bar Mariposa just pretended that she was dancing in
place a bit or at least feeling the rhythm as she stood
there, she churned her hips a little and kept smiling,
thinking about nothing but thinking about everything,
she made sort of a finger-snapping gesture with her two
hands dangling at her side, the music went on and on,
and hiply goateed Espíritu the disc jockey did little talking through his microphone, he didn't do much of anything except to play song after song and lean over occasionally from his perch on the low, black-painted turntable dais with its big speakers and complicated panel of
all kinds of buttons, switches, and lights, what seemed
like something from a rocket-launch center, Mariposa
sometimes thought, and Espíritu would lean over from
the dais to tug the headphones aside and listen to somebody request a song, he would nod, but he never let the
music stop, there was never a gap in between one song
and another, and no matter if it was *norteño* or *cumbia* it
went on and on, like the dream of working at El Pájaro

Verde, like the way that everything sometimes felt for Mariposa, she served a couple of more tables, and the place was definitely filling again now, Mr. Álvarez had been right, it was very hot for late October, as hot as July or August, and it was a Saturday night, the music was so loud, the smoke was getting thick and it smelled terrible, Mariposa knew that at home at her aunt's later she would put what she had worn, the top and the jeans, on a coat hanger to be placed outside the little window in that cramped back room where she slept with the two children, her cousins, she thought of later doing that, how she would have to air out her clothes, she thought of a lot of things, but then she suddenly was *very* busy, it could happen like that, there were suddenly many tables to take care of, there were tips to be made, and one time when she came back from a table with her tray she was surprised to find Carolina there with her friend Azul, the lesbian girl, they had just come in, they sat together at the bar, they were always very happy, and now they were happy to see her, Carolina tugged what could have been the rag doll of Mariposa close to her, gave her a hug, Azul called Mariposa *chica*, she looked right at Mariposa, she told Mariposa that she loved her eyes, *chica*, Mariposa laughed, Mariposa was really pleased to see them, it was good to have some-

body to talk to besides the men she had been taking orders from without even having one of them offer to buy
her a ten-dollar Tecate, but she knew for that to happen
you had to wait till a little later, when the men were
drunker, when they didn't care what they spent, that's
when you made money, more than on simple tips in a
job like this without any real salary, and that's when everything else at El Pájaro Verde became worthwhile for
Mariposa, when the job made at least some sense, she
had to earn money somehow, but now, yes, it was good
to have somebody to talk to while waiting for orders to
be filled at the bar besides the girls who worked as bartenders and who had to talk to you, or Fat Tommy who
sometimes did exchange a few words with Mariposa in
his slow, unassuming way if he came over to the bar to
ask the bartender to give him a Gatorade, Fat Tommy
liked Gatorade, orange Gatorade and not the dishwatery
green kind, he had once told her, so they kept several
bottles of it from a convenience store in the cooler, and
Mariposa wasn't sure she had the whole story on what
had happened, how exactly it worked with Carolina and
Azul, or how exactly *they* worked, and the way she
thought she understood it was that Carolina, who had
been employed regularly when Mariposa first started at
the club, she had managed to lose her job as a B-girl at

El Pájaro Verde, she was pretty, she had a round face, a
lovely moon, and hair cut wispy like feathers and dyed
with henna to make it look auburn, she always wore a
short skirt and never jeans with a top, maybe twenty-
three or twenty-four, she was slim with very pretty legs
that the short skirts displayed well, she had on a denim
skirt and a halter top tonight that looked tropical and
like something somebody would buy for a vacation,
white with a print of big turquoise palm trees at all crazy
angles on it, she had a tattoo of a boy's name in blue-
black gothic lettering sort of floating on one bare shoulder, she had a silver stud like a little snowdrop below
her lower lip, and Carolina had been a very, very popular
girl herself at Club El Pájaro Verde and had apparently
worked there for over a year before her girlfriend started
showing up, the lesbian girl the same age, Azul, who
had some kind of a good job in an office working for the
city, she was Mexican American, entirely legal, yes, apparently Carolina had been working at the club for
about a year before Azul began coming in to sit with her
at the bar like that, and if Carolina had that name of the
long-forgotten boy tattooed in the fancy letters in blue-
black on her smooth brown shoulder, that boy was surely long forgotten, as probably most boys were for Carolina, and now for Carolina there was Azul who looked

like a boy, who made no attempt to dress up and almost did just the opposite, who now wore boys' cargo shorts that drooped below her knees and a baggy green-and-brown camouflage shirt with the tails hanging out and an old faded ball cap, the visor hand-molded for the arc of a duck bill and tugged low, the front of it showing an embroidered Virgen de Guadalupe with a fan of gold rays emanating, Azul wearing that cap not necessarily out of any show of religion but maybe more so a funkily Latina in-your-face something that Azul was trying to tell people about, a La Raza kind of thing, Azul wore earrings, two little gold buttons like seashells that were perfect for her, so that with everything else very much making her look like a boy, the sloppy shorts, the sloppy camouflage shirt, the boys' old raggedy black canvas sneakers with no socks, her ankles themselves seeming a little dirty from walking around like that without socks, what the dainty gold earrings did was remind you that she was a girl and a pretty one, too, her upper lip would flatten over her slightly bucked teeth when she smiled, pretty, and when Carolina had worked as a B-girl at the club it apparently had begun, after a while Azul started showing up halfway through an evening to sit with Carolina at the bar and keep her company in between Carolina letting men buy her drinks, Carolina

and Azul chatting, laughing, then Carolina taking the
hand of one of the men who would lead her out to the
dance floor, dancing with him but always returning to
Azul at the bar, Carolina sometimes even sitting with
Azul on one side and a man on the other side, a man
who might buy her one of the little ten-dollar cans of
Tecate, the man putting his arm around her bare shoulders, because his ten dollars did entitle him to do that if
it was OK with the girl, Carolina listening to whatever
drunken whispering the man was going on with, turning
to him now and then and, as naturally as that, turning
back to Azul now and then, Azul sipping a bottle of beer
she paid for herself, the two girls chatting and laughing
some more, why, it was as if Carolina was being shared
by those on either side of her, it even got to a stage beyond that on a couple of Saturdays, and Mariposa had
seen this happen a few times, and as maybe a very fast
cumbia began, a song seeming more Colombian or Dominican than Mexican, its downbeat sounding and the
man sitting beside Carolina hearing it just then, the
man suggesting that they head out to the small dance
floor again, as that happened, there might be a moment
when Carolina did swivel off her stool, and Azul,
cranked up a little by the music, got up, too, she did the
same, swiveled off her stool, the two of them dancing

together a bit and really shaking their behinds together
there at the bar, shiveringly and rattlingly, belly-dancer
style, and staring at each other's behinds as they did it
and keeping it up through a quick few riffs of the song
for a moment, grinning at each other, happy in flaunting
their secret, maybe, and then Azul would hoist herself
back onto the bar stool to return to drinking her beer
while Carolina would continue out to the dance floor
with the man, the man waiting for her, silently watching, Mr. Álvarez didn't like it, he told Carolina that if
she had a girlfriend that was OK, that was her personal
life, but she shouldn't have her girlfriend with her while
at work in El Pájaro Verde, apparently he was businesslike about it and firm, the way that Mr. Álvarez in the
light blue *guayabera* and with his bald pate glossy under
the meticulously arranged black strands combed straight
back could be businesslike and firm on just about everything, and while Mr. Álvarez knew that somebody like
Mariposa wasn't even twenty-one and that according to
state law she could be *serving* drinks but not *consuming*
them, he had been just that, businesslike and firm,
when he had first hired her and told her that if anybody
asked her about her drinking the tiny can of Tecate, she
was supposed to deny it, she was supposed to say that
she wasn't drinking but just serving, the trick was never

to be caught actually drinking, which meant *consuming*, and Mariposa had learned the name they called the inspectors, "TABC men," who she pictured as wearing dark suits and dark sunglasses, like secret agents, but who of course didn't dress that way and who, in truth, never did seem to show at any of these clubs, what went on in East Austin was East Austin's own concern, or that was probably how the TABC men saw it, and Mr. Álvarez had told Carolina repeatedly that she shouldn't be sitting there with her girlfriend like that, it was all too obvious and it didn't look right to have the pair of them together like that, he made it an ultimatum, until Carolina didn't show one night, and word among the girls had it that Carolina had simply changed clubs, gone down the street to work as a B-girl at Bar Texas, taking Azul with her, and now Carolina was talking to Mariposa, now Mariposa was so pleased to see her again, Mariposa stood there with the two girls who sat facing her on the stools, she liked Carolina and Azul, they were fun and she hadn't seen them for a couple of weeks, and what all the other girls knew, and what Mr. Álvarez eventually learned more than anybody else, was that Mr. Álvarez had made a mistake, and the men who showed up and who regularly sat with Carolina, those who regularly bought her beer after beer and danced

with Carolina in the short skirts that showed off her legs
so well, the sculpted calves of them slight at the ankle,
the sculpted thighs of them higher up, the men kept
asking Mr. Álvarez what had happened to her, Mr. Álvarez lied and said he had no idea, he said that probably
she had left town, and then Mr. Álvarez learned that
some of those men had started frequenting Bar Texas in
what was once the old redbrick hotel down the street
and that had a half-dozen pool tables, true, several regulars who had formerly come to El Pájaro Verde now
went there, not to put in a leisurely hour or so of long
bilar sticks chalked and the balls perpetually click-click-
ing for a couple of games at a table, but to find Carolina, it turned out, and as all the girls at El Pájaro Verde
knew, men, or at least some men, liked the idea of having Carolina sit between one of them and Azul at the
bar, Carolina even being pawed by the man and then by
Azul, Carolina pivoting on the stool this way for a bit
and then that way for a bit, Carolina being *really* shared,
pawed sometimes by *both* at the same time, and those
men probably liked seeing the two girls get up and rattle
their behinds together so fast, so crazily, enough to out-
do the pop singer Shakira who herself could seem
hooked up to electricity, Mariposa sometimes thought,
wild voltage, the way Shakira shook, the men liked the

little show of two girls dancing like that for a few very loud cascading notes from the big speakers, before the man, whoever he might be, would lead Carolina out to the dance floor again, it seemed to be a turn-on, which is to say, Mr. Álvarez had lost some business, he wanted Carolina back at Club El Pájaro Verde, and he wanted her along with wise-cracking and sometimes gruff Azul included in the package, and Carolina now explained to Mariposa that she was here this Saturday night to talk to him about maybe doing just that, Mr. Álvarez had gone as far as to suggest he was willing to give a better cut than usual on each overpriced drink Carolina sold, she and Azul had walked over from Bar Texas a few blocks down the cracked sidewalk during Carolina's break, and Carolina told Mariposa that Bar Texas wasn't the same as Club El Pájaro Verde, she made as much money but she didn't like some of the people there, she said the problem was that while just blocks away, Bar Texas was, nevertheless, very different, she didn't like the two brothers who owned the place at all, and everybody there, especially those two crazy brothers, was obsessed lately with break-ins after some kids had climbed up from outside and yanked out a window air-conditioner built into the wall of the club and somehow crawled in though the high opening to steal a few

bottles of whiskey after closing time, Carolina got tired
of hearing everybody at Bar Texas talk about that, they
only talked about that, the robbery, it could have been
news of a new world war or a massive atomic bomb being dropped, as far as the two brothers were concerned,
and, worse, sometimes Bar Texas felt more like what it
really was, a pool hall rather than a dance club, and
Azul sarcastically added something along the lines of
Bar Texas being in essence, yes, a pool hall, but even as
such it was one with the chief featured entertainment
being *borrachos* vomiting on the tables, and Carolina,
laughing much more, told Mariposa that Mariposa
wouldn't believe it, Carolina kept laughing, she said that
exactly *that* had happened one night, a man *totalmente*
borracho, or maybe *bien apija,* as Mariposa's Honduran
brother would say, the man simply got up from his chair,
walked over to a pool table where two guys were playing
a game, one of the players maybe lining up a tough angle shot with the cue ball aimed ever so perfectly for the
anticipated ricochet, and the drunkard proceeded to
simply lean over and vomit extensively and continuously
on the pool table's green felt, Carolina said that's the
kind of place Bar Texas was, a place where the loss of a
few lousy bottles of whiskey was earth-shattering news,
where a man had once volcanically vomited on a pool

table, it was different than El Pájaro Verde, and Mariposa laughed, and then Mariposa noticed that Azul was staring straight at her, Mariposa, as Mariposa listened to Carolina, Azul studying Mariposa, seemingly mesmerized by what she saw, Azul said to her in English, "Those eyes, they drive me crazy," and hearing that, Carolina slapped Azul's thigh as you might a disobedient or naughty child, just said "Chica!," and Azul laughed, said back to her the same, "Chica!," then gave her a harder slap on the denim of Carolina's tiny skirt, her thigh, all three of them laughed, Mariposa still standing, the two girls on the stools, and then Azul was more serious, she told Mariposa outright that she seemed too bright to be working a job like this, and Azul was Mexican American, and Azul had that good job in an office of the City of Austin, and even if she only did photocopying there, maybe, or even if she only stuffed letters in a mailroom, she had that kind of a good job, she was Mexican American, Tejano, and she knew about things, because being Mexican American was different than being somebody who came across the border for work, the paths of the two groups seemed to seldom cross, if truth be known, never mind what could often feel like the sizable distance away from the white world for *both* groups, and Azul could give advice like a teacher, an Anglo, let's say, and it was almost as if that even with pretty, moon-faced Carolina sitting right there in her denim skirt and tropical top, her hair smelling wonderfully like coconut from shampooing, the fact that Azul had said that Mariposa was too bright to be working there, which might possibly suggest that Carolina herself wasn't very bright, it didn't offend Carolina, Carolina was where she was supposed to be, actually, working as a B-girl, so it all seemed to have been lost on Carolina, who probably didn't care if she was considered bright or not, but she didn't exactly appreciate her own girlfriend admiring another girl's admittedly pretty eyes, repeatedly complimenting about them, the amber eyes accentuated by Mariposa's complexion of such a rich caramel hue and her lustrous black hair, long hair brushed back from her temples in that simple style, eyes like hers were indeed very rare, and in a hesitant voice, quietly, Mariposa told Azul in Spanish that she had to learn more English, Azul looked up from under the blue baseball cap's duck bill, she had those little gold shells for earrings, Azul agreed with Mariposa that she should do that, work on her English, and Azul again like a schoolteacher and entirely serious told her, yes, she *really* needed English, it was important, and Mariposa told her again how she realized that to be true, Mariposa said her brother in

Tennessee had told her the same, her brother had gone out of his way to learn English, fast, he had no trouble with it, and Azul told Mariposa that her brother had been wise to do so, that was good, Carolina nodded, agreeing wholeheartedly with the advice herself, but any conversation among the girls about language didn't have time to go much beyond such emphatic general agreement, because all three of them looked to the door now, and there Fat Tommy, droopy-eyed as ever, was holding up his orange flashlight like a baton to get their attention above the other heads, he was in the open doorway motioning for Carolina, which meant that Mr. Álvarez was waiting in his office up the creaky outside wooden stairs and above the club and that Carolina could go there and talk to him now, Mr. Álvarez would see her now, both she and Azul hugged Mariposa before they left, and they did leave together, would surely go into Mr. Álvarez's office together, to talk about Carolina coming back to work for Mr. Álvarez, it was funny, and Mariposa brought more beers to more tables, Club El Pájaro Verde was becoming very crowded, and Mariposa thought of everything and she thought of nothing, La canción de Mariposa, everything and nothing at all, and what she thought about was what she had already thought about, or maybe it was what she hadn't even already thought about, it was what she was yet to think about, so many things, because time could get completely shuffled, that was how it worked in the dream of Club El Pájaro Verde (*how did that go before? was there moonlight in her town in Honduras even now, and did the white alcaldía in the square amidst the neat palm trees still show its clock on top, a clock with big black roman numerals and ornate black hands trying to tell the time to anybody if he or she were willing to listen, trying to whisper it with the chiming of the hour, the long, lingering, but always so soft, metal notes that hung in the sweet and very fragrant air of her town in Honduras? was there the maybe admitted absolute futility of all those fluttering money telegrams, yellow and black from Western Union, still beating their way like butterflies southward over the mountains and deserts and jungles in the moonlight, going there but never getting there, because did anything really ever go anywhere, get anywhere . . . and it was all the same, but could it all, someday, be somehow different?*), which is when she did notice the Anglo man at the bar, and maybe he had already been sitting there at the end of the bar while she had been talking with Carolina and Azul, maybe she just hadn't noticed him sitting there alone, or maybe he had come in while she was busy and off bringing beers to yet another table, always making sure to lift napkins from the tray to wrap one around each of the brown bottles, and . . .

. . . and Mariposa saw him there (later she might tell herself she *didn't* see him sitting there), she saw him sitting on a stool looking out at everything, taking it all in, the Anglo man (but she *did* see him sitting there), he was smiling, she was heading back to the bar with her tray, and it was as if Inés must have spotted him at the same time, the Anglo alone and without a *copa*, and there seemed to be some hesitation, or confusion, because it was up to a girl to work fast, nobody had a set area or set tables, and if you wanted to just sit around and talk with other girls and occasionally answer your cell phone at a table that was OK, or if you wanted to sit around and mindlessly touch your finger to the glowing electronic screen of the game called video poker, trying to look bored like that, as if you didn't care about making money no matter what Mr. Álvarez wanted, that was OK, too, but otherwise you had to work fast, though somehow in looking back on it, for Mariposa, it wasn't just working fast this time, every girl knew the universal

verb "hustle" and what it meant at any of the clubs on
East Sixth Street, that was one word that didn't need
any translation, but this was different, and Inés was already up, she was already tugging down a little on each
side of the tight white Wranglers at her full hips, where
the jeans had ridden up as she sat, the jeans that tapered and that were rolled a couple of times at her
calves for neat cuffs that made them look pegged, that
made her seem even more top-heavy, if possible, than
she actually was on her clear plastic high heels, the
scarlet elasticized tube top suggesting maybe a flower
fully blossoming above the stem of the jeans, the silver
cell phone like some absurd mechanical eye of the flower and now placed smack in the center of the scarlet
tube top, the cell phone nestled in the shadowy cleft,
the bulgingly ample flesh of her, and Inés tugged up on
each side of the tube top, under one arm and then the
other, pulled the whole thing up a little, then she passed
her fingers, three of them held together in sort of an in-
advertent salute gesture, across that wing of black hair
that fell to one side, almost over her eye completely, almost clear to the tiny stud piercing her nose, she
pushed the flap of hair aside some, like a crow's wing,
maybe, very glossy and very black, to see better through
both eyes, the long lashes of them that Inés was proud

of, glistening with Vaseline so they looked even longer, so they looked wet, Inés who did have those pretty dimples in her cheeks when she smiled, maybe she pushed the hair aside that way to see exactly where she was going, see exactly what her target was, because it was as if she spotted the Anglo sitting at the bar at the same time Mariposa did, Mariposa was returning from the tables beside the dance floor, Mariposa spotted him, or simply saw him, and you could have made a funny Saturday-morning cartoon of it, it was like something in those crazy TV cartoons that her two little cousins howled about on Saturday morning at the rented place on Chicón Street, and coming from one side was Inés and coming from the other side was Mariposa, on a slapstick collision course, even though maybe it wasn't *quite* like that, and Mariposa was probably surprised herself that she made such an effort on it, and it wasn't as if she elbowed Inés out of the way or anything, but she did look right at the Anglo who was smiling, and, smiling herself, Mariposa headed right toward him, and her behavior now could have been due to that entire scenario earlier and the pure meanness of Inés having done what she did then, scattering the napkins like that, brushing them in a sweep so some even fluttered to the dirty floor for Mariposa to have to pick them up there, and in a way

that kept Mariposa going now, made her very determined, she had to be brave, there had been *no* reason
for Inés to do that except that Inés knew that she certainly *could* do it, she was Mexican and Mariposa was
Honduran, the men liked Mariposa and Inés certainly
didn't like the fact that they did like her (on the other
hand, Mariposa couldn't help but feel bad for Inés, and
Inés, despite her never-ending bossiness, despite her
being more or less the ringleader of the smug, catty girls
who always sat with her at her table, especially Carmen,
Inés would soon enough end up, Mariposa knew, as
only one of those flabby, sagging, thick-legged older
women, like *las tres mujeres*, with worn-out eyes and
splotched skin and dull sparse hair, wearing too much
eye-liner and too much smeared lipstick, even fishnet
stockings with runs, Inés becoming just one of those
women who talked to the men as if mothers, there was
nothing for Inés, really, and it was common knowledge
that Inés did go out to the back parking lot with men,
that she did things to them when they unbuckled their
belt and zipped open the fly of their jeans in a pickup
truck or the back seat of a car there in the shadows under the brace of spreading live oak trees behind the lit
taquería trailer that smelled of its charcoal fires for the
burnt fajitas, the trailer that had the display of fruit so-

das in clear-glass bottles that shone luridly, near phan-
tasmagorically, green and orange and red, the lined-up
bottles like neon in that glaring light of the open-sided
silver trailer, and maybe that was why Inés didn't have
to "hustle" in the bar all the time, she could sit at the
table even more casually than the other girls, she made
her real money in other ways, but once, that one time,
Mariposa had seen Inés in the Damas after Inés had
come back from the parking lot, Inés was crying there in
the ladies' room, she was scooping up handfuls of water
from the cracked porcelain sink and splashing it on her
face and crying, not caring if she was ruining her makeup, coughing some and spitting out the water some, and
crying some more, the faucet kept running and running,
and Mariposa might have thought about backing off
now, Mariposa might have felt bad for Inés, Mariposa
really didn't care about what Inés had done with the
napkins, Mariposa even felt stupid for trying to be so
conscientious, for even doing something like the careful
arranging of the napkins during the time she had to kill
there at the bar before the place filled up, Club El Pájaro Verde, it was all useless, it was all nothing but a
dream, but maybe she didn't think of *any* of that), and
Mariposa was nonchalantly tapping the tray as she
walked, bobbing a little to the music booming, yes, tap-

ping the brown plastic tray with her unpainted finger-
nails as if it was a big tambourine, as naturally and nonchalantly as that, but she didn't let her eyes wander
from the Anglo's eyes now looking right at her (though it
could have been that she had no choice, and it was all
more than inevitable, but it was crazy to believe that,
and it just happened, and, really, there was no time to
think of the futility of Inés's life and no time to even
wonder, as she might have later wondered, *what if* she
hadn't kept going toward the man, *what if* she had
bumped into a couple of other men coming into the
packed place through the front door and stopped to take
their order, or, more so, maybe Inés might have moved
faster and gotten to him before Mariposa did, as Mariposa simply let Inés get to him first, though, again, it
probably was true that Mariposa had no choice, it *had*
to happen), Mariposa was now standing in front of the
man, and nobody had asked him if he wanted a beer,
and he wasn't actually sitting at the bar but on a bar
stool a bit beyond the end of the bar, beside the little
counter of sorts along the wall, no wider than a board
and like a shelf, where there were more of the bar
stools, it turned out that she had more English than he
had Spanish, but he seemed to know what she meant
when Mariposa smiled and asked him if he would like a

copa, she smiled very wide, Inés was gone, most likely
Inés had just turned around or told herself it wasn't
worth the effort, the Anglo seemed to know what *copa*
meant, and he said in a slow, twanging Western drawl,
"Una cerveza Budweiser, sure, darlin'," he wasn't that
young, probably in his fifties, a tall, rugged, cowboyish
man in pretty good shape, with short gray hair and
tanned though leathery, he smiled, wearing jeans and a
Western shirt unbuttoned low so you could see some of
the gray hair on his chest, no hat, and . . .

. . . and he had given her a twenty-dollar bill,
Mariposa waited for Toni the bartender to get the Budweiser and open it, then she waited for Toni to make
change for Mariposa, and Mariposa brought the beer on
the tray over to the man, she placed the tray on the
shelf along the wall, under more posters for Corona and
Negra Modelo and Tecate, those buxom, sultry-eyed,
full-lipped girls posing on palm-treed beaches with the
aqua sea behind them, wearing ridiculously scant bikinis, wearing Western hats, he himself went to lift the
beer off the tray and she smiled, told him pleasantly,

"No," as he slowly pulled back his reaching hand and watched as Mariposa carefully picked up the cheap white paper napkin, thin, she carefully unfolded it and then took the little blanket of the thing and wrapped it around the longneck brown bottle of Budweiser, using both hands to mold it close to the sweating bottle like that, the napkin damp now and very easily molded, Mariposa cupping it as if a potter at work to get it all right, flattened all around the bottle, then picking the bottle up before she handed it to him and using her fingers to tap the napkin along the edges at the bottom, too, opening her palm to flatten the napkin better there with a couple of firmer pats so it would sit right when he put the bottle down, she could make a bottle of beer look like something precious, she knew how to do that, and he said, "That's a good idea, that's a very good idea on a hot night like this, darlin'," and he did say "darlin'" a lot, he smiled when he said it, she handed him the beer, she took the seventeen dollars in change from the tray and slowly and aloud counted it out in Spanish as she handed it to him, three fives and two ones, "Cinco, diez, quince" for the fives and then lingering on the syllables, "Di-e-ci-séis, di-e-ci-si-et-e," for the ones, he looked down to the flap pocket on the front of the beige-checked Western shirt, it had a little pearl snap button on it, he unsnapped it and poked the fives in the pocket, handed the two ones to her, "That's for you, dar-lin'," he said, Mariposa took the money, folded the bills in half and slipped them in the back pocket of her jeans, snug there and showing the shape of her behind, those pockets that she had embroidered herself in squiggly red and gold and green, swirling leaf and floral designs, they started talking some, he said that he flew helicopters, he wasn't from Austin and he was here on a job, he said that he had never been in El Pájaro Verde before, had never even been in Austin before, he just happened to have had dinner at a Mexican place on this side of town, El Azteca Restaurant, the clerk at the mo-tel where he was staying told him about the restaurant, recommended it, told him the East Side was best for Mexican food, then he had been driving around, he saw the club, thought he might stop in for a beer on such a hot night, and there was something about him as soon as he told Mariposa that he flew helicopters that made her think that, yes, he looked like a pilot or at least some kind of a military man, or Mariposa thought that he looked like he had been in the Army, in pretty good shape at his age, tanned like that, the short-cropped gray hair, yes, for some reason she told him that he looked like he was in the military, and he repeated that

he flew helicopters for clients now, and, true, he had
been in the military, "But that was way back when, a
long, long time ago," he was there by himself, he patted
the red plastic top of the stool next to him and Mariposa
looked at it, she hoisted herself up onto it, and if a man
gave you a good tip you could sit with him for a few
minutes, he didn't always have to pay for a ten-dollar
Tecate for you to talk with him, she hoisted herself up
and eased her behind fully onto the stool and hooked
the two flat heels of the dressy beige sandals on its rusted chrome rung, she thought about the lime-green halter top, wanted to reach up and adjust it some, those
flaps that tied for the bow in front of the thing, but she
didn't, he told her his name was Bill, she told him her
name was Mariposa, and that was the way it began, they
continued talking, bouncing words in both languages
back and forth some, like ping-pong balls, until each
understood the other, more or less, laughing about their
mistakes with words, and they communicated OK, it
was easier to talk in this part of the club, not as loud,
and she explained to him that Mariposa meant butterfly,
he nodded, smiled, he said it was a pretty name, she
asked him where he flew helicopters, he said just about
everywhere lately, "I started flying choppers when I
wasn't much more than a kid, probably wouldn't know

how to do anything else now, darlin','" and Mariposa
asked him to say it again, that word, and he asked her
what word, and she said the word he had just said, this
Anglo man named Bill, the word he had used for a helicopter, he said "What?" and she said "La palabra" and
then corrected herself and said "La word," and he said
"Chopper?," and a bit excited she told him that was *it,*
and it would be a good word to learn, Mariposa knew,
she had never heard that word before, and she tried it
herself, she said "Chopper" almost like a child would
repeat a new word just learned, careful to get the "ch" of
it right, then her fresh lips that didn't even need lipstick
fluttering on the two *p*'s of it and her very fresh, translu-
cently white teeth bright in her smile and showing again
for the "er" that really came out more like the Spanish
"rr," trilled yet clipped, this Bill told her she was cute
when she said that, he asked her to say it again, she said
"No," but smiling all the while, and she told him again
that she didn't have much English, she told him he
probably thought it was funny the way she had just said
that word, and he said, no, he thought it was *cute,*
"You're cute when you say that, darlin'," and somewhat
embarrassed she told him again, "No!," still smiling good
naturedly, they both laughed, he sipped his beer (the
police in Albuquerque and Phoenix knew, of course,

that he did have a way about him with girls, they also
knew that he sometimes used that same concocted story with girls, saying he flew helicopters), and she tried
to explain some things to him, things that he asked
about out of curiosity, he seemed interested in everything she had to say, she told him that she had worked
at the club for about a month, she told him about Honduras, she told him what the capital city was, Tegucigalpa, which he said he knew about, at least the name,
and she told him where her town was, not too far from
Tegucigalpa and in the mountains, a very beautiful
town, he said that he himself had heard Honduras was a
beautiful country indeed, or that's what Mariposa
thought he said, and he said that he spoke "only muy
poquito español," and in most of the talk they had to
rely on more of that bouncing back and forth of words,
those little, repeatedly popping, yes, ping-pong balls, the
volleyed syllables, it all nearly turned into charades at
times, and he would often say "Cómo se dice en español?" and she would tell him, and he said that now that
he thought of it, the two most important phrases he
knew in Spanish were maybe exactly the two that he
had just used, they were the most important ones, "muy,
muy poquito," about the amount of Spanish he did
have, and "Cómo se dice en español?," which he said

had always been what saved him when it came to Spanish, but despite all that, they did manage to talk, have a conversation, laughing some more, and he drained what was left in his brown Budweiser bottle in a tilting, extended swig, rolling his gray eyes back when he did it, saying afterwards, "That's cold beer, that's good on a hot night like this," and she explained to him that even while it wasn't that hot right now inside Club El Pájaro Verde, it could have been cooler, she explained that the front door to the sidewalk and the street was always kept open, men outside liked to look in a club, they liked to see what was going on before they came in, though she wasn't quite sure if he understood that, what she said, it was complicated for Mariposa to explain it mostly in Spanish but some English, too, she really had to learn English, speak it better, she knew, that was what her brother had told her, that was what Azul had just told her, though Azul had also said something else, about computers, how computers were important to know about, though Mariposa should have told Azul again that English was the most important thing to her now, and maybe she didn't even want to think about computers because, in a way, computers reminded her of Tennessee, the city called Nashville in Tennessee, where it was cold, where it snowed and where it wasn't

supposed to snow, there were mountains around the
city, but not the gentle green mountains of Honduras,
all verdant groves and splashing waterfalls and bright
tropical birds noisily chirping and cawing, trading their
important secrets in the humid, sun-drenched beauty of
it all, and the mountains beyond the few skyscrapers
that made for the downtown of the city called Nashville
were bleak, they were somehow black with no leaves on
the trees in winter, or maybe the bare trees on the
mountains looked like just so much aimless black pencil
scribbling, cold, her brother assured her that snow like
that, real snow, deep, was actually rare for Tennessee,
but the snow did come, the biggest storm lasted two full
days, cold, the flakes were sometimes fine and blowing
as if blasted, so many tiny exploding diamonds in the
streetlight when, huddled against the biting wind, Mariposa would have to walk to the 7-Eleven from her
brother's apartment to buy a gallon jug of milk and a loaf
of white sandwich bread for the family in the snow, then
sometimes the flakes were thick, flakes very large and
floppy, big enough to be moths fluttering under those
streetlights, cold, she didn't want to think about Tennessee, she had bought a cheap pink nylon parka at the
second-hand store called Bargains Plus that was really
sort of a Salvation Army store with a different kind of

name, but it did little good, she was always shivering, Mariposa never thought she could be that cold, Austin was better, or it was warmer, anyway, and for her, to think about computers, the subject Azul had brought up, was also to admit that she, Mariposa, had gotten outright fired from the job at Completely Wired, the computer-supply chain store, she hadn't even been there a full two weeks in the shipping room with all the others, working fast to assemble the boxes that came flat and had to be assembled for packing, working fast to the shrill screeching of the rolls of wide brown plastic tape yanked to seal up the boxes in the packing, she worked as fast and as hard as anybody else, she didn't want to disappoint her brother who had the good job driving a delivery van for Completely Wired and who had gotten her a job, too, who had told her to come up from Honduras and she could live with him and his family while she got started on the job, but she needed better English, she didn't understand what the supervisor was telling her, she didn't understand what came out on the so-called memos printed on long canary-yellow sheets with updates on new postal policies and new packaging regulations, she was fired, then she worked at the Burger King in Nashville, they would hire anybody at the Burger King, and she didn't show the Anglo the scars at first, no, she didn't, and Mariposa knew that at some point she would have to learn more about computers but for the moment she really needed to learn English better, and after she accomplished that who knew what could happen, she had a good education, for Honduras, anyway, she had gone to the technical high school there in her town for almost three years, Mariposa in her school uniform of plain white blouse and plain blue skirt, her boyfriend back then was the one who had made the belt for her, the tooled leather belt with her name in turquoise and yellow and with the white butterflies fluttering, he was named Alejandro, but that was very long ago, he was just a boy, it wasn't anything serious, and if she had better English she could maybe take courses at Austin Community College, this was America not Honduras, anything could happen here, she could take courses like Fat Tommy was doing, Mariposa, and sometimes she was thinking of everything, sometimes of nothing at all, and she looked at the bottle of Budweiser that the Anglo named Bill had now placed down on the little shelf behind him as the two of them sat there on the red-topped bar stools (the police also knew that he used different names, there was never one name, and there was never a pattern to the names, set aliases with a traceable connection, they had no idea how many names he actually used, those police in both Phoenix and Albuquerque who, just a month before, had intensified their efforts and assembled a joint squad to work on all of this), and he had finished his beer, the napkin was by that point thoroughly soggy, a disintegrating white pulp on the brown longneck bottle, "Una otra?" she asked him, and he said, "Sure, darlin', an otra cerveza," and he told her to get a drink for herself, too, he was already fingering the flap on the beige check shirt to unsnap the pearl button, to tug out the bills, the three fives, Mariposa was up off the stool, she was standing there smiling, almost standing at attention, and he simply handed her all the bills, again paying before she even left, he was looking right at her, he asked her a question that seemed to be if anybody had ever told her that she had pretty eyes, or she thought that was what he said, because he then said, "Cómo se dice eyes en español?," and even with the bills in her hand she was able to make a spread *V* with her fingers as if she was going to poke her own eyes but was only pointing to them, "Los ojos," she said, and he said that he should have known that, he remembered the word now, and now he repeated it as if he was the one patiently learning the lesson, "Los ojos," and she said, "Perfecto!," she headed toward the bar, walking away, and often when she took an order from a man at a table and walked away, she was self-conscious, because she knew, of course, she knew that as soon as she would turn around a man would be looking at the roundness of her small behind in the snug jeans with the embroidery on the two pockets, and she knew that on a night like this when she had worn the lime-green halter top that left her shoulders and nearly her entire back bare that the men would also be studying the uncovered flesh, the nakedness of her, as men do, but for some reason she didn't think of that happening with this Anglo named Bill, and he seemed very friendly, he seemed different, and waiting at the bar, listening to the song from Los Tigres del Norte, a favorite that seemed to get everybody up to dance, she glanced around some, Fat Tommy was still in the doorway, she saw him lackadaisically scratch the back of his uniform shirt with the long day-glo orange plastic flashlight, then he was staring out to the street again, the men constantly passing, going this way and that, and the table with Inés and Carmen and the other girls was at last empty, which meant that they must have all been dancing, any song from Los Tigres del Norte made men want to dance, to be with somebody out there on the patch of linoleum under the pulsating red light, Club El Pájaro Verde was reaching the peak of its night, when it was most crowded at ten-thirty or so, Toni the bartender was getting the Budweiser and the squat can of Tecate, a can like a little red barrel, more or less a parody of a full beer, Toni put the drinks on Mariposa's tray, and when Mariposa walked back to the Anglo, smiling some more as she approached, she looked around at least enough to check if Ignacio in his black Stetson and fine black Western clothes was there with his *compadres*, but he hadn't come, she lifted the drinks off the tray, she wrapped a napkin around his beer, she took the two one-dollar bills from the tray to hand to him and he frowned, waved them away, and she wanted to tell him that he didn't have to give her a two-dollar tip now, explain to him that men who came to a place like Club El Pájaro Verde or Club El Indio or Club Tío Raúl's, they all knew that when you bought a girl a beer for ten dollars she didn't expect a tip, she was making her money on the ten-dollar beer, a beer that Mariposa would hardly sip, it was more or less a token, a stage prop, but she didn't explain that to him, she knew that he would have argued with her anyway, told her to keep the tip, and after he took a first sip of his beer and when the song of Los Tigres del Norte had finished and a new one began, a Mexican *cumbia*, he said that he had heard that song

before, the last one, he said that while he really knew
nothing about this sort of music, it was one song that he
had seemed to have heard on the radio, when driving,
maybe, and she explained why he probably had, and
again it was like when she explained other things, talked
to him about the air-conditioner trying to hissingly do its
best in the club though it was difficult to keep the place
cool, seeing that the front door had to be left open, and
if anybody working at the club complained that the air-
conditioner would have had a better chance of cooling if
the door was kept closed, Mr. Álvarez always said again
that men expected the front door to be left open, men
wanted to look inside before they entered, and Mariposa herself knew that even back in Honduras the *can-
tinas* for men that she would hurriedly pass by when on
her way to or from school always had a set of louvered
saloon doors, half-doors that you could see over easily
enough, so they made for an open door of sorts, too, yes,
she had tried to explain the policy in detail to the Anglo
man, and when he said now that he had heard the song
that had just played, heard it somewhere before, Mariposa understood him, and back up on the stool beside
him, she told him that it wasn't surprising, Los Tigres
del Norte were popular, they were probably the most
famous group for the music called *norteño*, them and

maybe Los Tucanes de Tijuana, and while the word *tigre* was easy enough for him to understand, the word *tucán* was more difficult, because while Mariposa knew what it meant, a *tucán* was a tropical bird, a big beak, this Anglo named Bill was having trouble getting the idea of it despite the English equivalent being similar, and she knew the word for bird in English and she told him, yes, a *tucán* was "a bird," and the word for bird in Spanish was "a pájaro," but she wanted to make sure that he didn't think it was yet another kind of bird, one altogether different, like an eagle or even a buzzard, a *tucán* was special and for these singers it was even different than just the usual idea of a big-beaked *tucán,* the group were songbirds, she tried to say, that's the way everybody thought of them, true songbirds, and then she put down her own can of beer on the shelf and puckered her lips and sucked in her cheeks and titled her head this way and that some, perkily, as if pantomiming maybe a lark now, a songbird, she even whistled a little as she did it, and while he maybe still didn't quite get the implication, he did say, "That's cute, that's really cute when you do that, darlin'," she tried to explain that with Mexican *norteño* music you almost had to declare your allegiance to one band or the other, it was like having a favorite *fútbol* team, Los Tigres del Norte were more

serious, gruffer, there was a lot in their songs that was
about the lives of *indocumentados* and also politics,
while Los Tucanes were usually more light-hearted,
happy, their songs might have the same drums and accordion and guitars of all *norteño*, but their songs were
more about parties and girls and motorcycles and the
beach, also love songs, that sort of thing, even if they
sometimes sang *narcocorridos*, and he did seem to follow
some of it, he said that it might be like the two camps
for fans when he was younger, he said that either you
had to like the Beatles or you had to like the Rolling
Stones, and he said that the Beatles, or at least the
songs of the singer Paul McCartney, were always more
lighthearted, the Beatles always had more love songs,
cheery, while the Rolling Stones were rougher, more serious sometimes, maybe like growling tigers, she said
that she knew about the Beatles and the Rolling Stones,
of course, even if she had no real idea of the exact difference between them that he was trying to explain, she
didn't tell him that, he asked her again what kind of bird
she was trying to tell him about, "A parrot?" and she
said, "No!" it wasn't a parrot, a parrot was a *papagayo*, or
it could actually be a *pájaro verde*, the name of the club
itself, this kind of bird was different, and so what kind
of bird was it, he asked her, or, more exactly, what was

the band like, how did they sound, and Mariposa puckered her lips again, she tilted her head this way and that again, perkily, bobbingly, to try to tell him about the singers, she whistled some again, hopefully a songbird's chirpy music, and when he said again "That's really, really cute," she knew that he had tricked her into doing it again, this time she lightly slapped him on the knee of his jutting leg as if to scold him, Mariposa putting on a mock knitting of the eyebrows, a definite frown, and probably she hadn't noticed herself doing that either, touching the man's knee again, and while Mr. Álvarez had been straightforward in instructing every girl that she should expect a man to put his arm around her if he bought her a beer, that she should expect his hands to move around some if they were on the dance floor, those hands that could feel as coarse as tree bark, as rough as pebbles in the street, the touch that Mariposa sometimes did hate so much, Mr. Álvarez had also suggested that it sometimes was good to even casually touch a man yourself when you wanted to make a point about something in the course of conversation, that relaxed a man, a relaxed man spent more money, which meant more money for both the girl and the club, but now she hadn't even noticed herself doing it, and more than once she had put her hand on his knee or thigh during the conversation as they sat there on the stools, she was already very relaxed with him, it was OK, and they continued to talk like that, it was almost part of her own song, her life now in this year that was somehow 2005, Mariposa far away from home, La canción de Mariposa, they talked about Honduras some more, and for some reason in the course of it then, Mariposa again put down the beer that she had still hardly sipped and she used two hands to lift up the necklace she wore, she gazed down her own snub nose and used those maybe very rare light hazel eyes to look right at the little gold cross that she lifted in both hands, a gesture somehow childish, too, to tell him, proudly, that she was católica, the cross had been given to her by her abuelita in her town beyond Tegucigalpa, it always brought her luck, she told him, and in saying that she maybe did have a remembered glimpse again of the crazy way she had just walked across the border, as easily as that, nobody would ever believe it, people talked about crackdowns at the border and of interrogations, even spoke of valid passports that were supposed to be required within the next year or so, but there had been none of that for Mariposa, she had been lucky, she now held the little gold cross, he asked her how you said "Mass" in Spanish and she understood that, she told him "Misa," and he

asked her if she went to Mass, and she told him that,
yes, sometimes, she went with her aunt, Tía Gloria and
her children, to the church that you could see if you
went to the door here at the club, you probably *could*
look out and see it in the blue moonlight, the lumpy rise
of it just blocks away and its bell tower in the oddly me-
dieval Spanish style, Iglesia Cristo Rey, Christ the King
Church it was, and she explained to him that everybody
was Mexican at the church, though maybe a few Asians,
too, from Vietnam, she thought, she said that this part
of the East Side, an older enclave of Austin itself, was
mostly Mexican, but it was changing, people told her
that, and she said that while the clubs were here, yes,
while the clubs were here where the old Mexican clubs
had always been, on East Sixth Street, that was changing, too, Mariposa's aunt herself told Mariposa about
the difference now, or people who had lived here in
East Austin for a long time often told Mariposa's aunt
about it, she said, and she, Mariposa, hadn't even been
here much more than a month, she explained to him
again, she of course didn't have firsthand knowledge
herself, but the Mexican neighbors told her aunt that
everything was rapidly changing, there were still the
tumbledown houses, sometimes divided up into apart-
ments and with worn dirt yards surrounded by bent

chain-link fence, those dogs always barking, houses like
the one where her aunt rented on Chicón, but outsiders
were buying up property, would probably soon buy the
bars as well, put them out of business, and most Mexicans who came here to the bars and nightclubs now did,
in fact, live elsewhere, maybe just because there were
so many more Mexicans in Austin now, though she
knew it would be far too complicated to explain to him
the whole other world that for her and others like her
wasn't even one of Mexican Americans, the world that
wasn't even Austin or Texas *or* the Estados Unidos, and
for *indocumentados* Austin's sleek skyline itself of glassy
towers was often but an imagined City of Oz, nothing to
do with the distinct and entirely separate world of the
*indocumentado*s who would remain *indocumentado*s, different laws wouldn't ever change anything, *ever,* or they
wouldn't change anything except the rules that nobody
really cared about, anyway, there were the new outlying
barrios of flimsy apartment housing that turned shabby
ten years after it was slapped up, Dove Springs and a lot
of East Riverside and Oltorf, there was the open-air
mercado on Pleasant Valley Road where you just as well
be in the middle of Mexico itself, and he seemed to understand some of that, too, he said that driving around
that night and coming back from El Azteca Restaurant,

admittedly a tourist spot, he said that he had seen some "redevelopment," and while he himself didn't know much about Austin, he could tell that property like this just across and under the elevated Interstate 35 and so close to the downtown of a booming city like Austin could in time become very valuable, and then Mariposa admitted, guiltily, thinking about church again, she said that she didn't go to Mass as much as she should, she admitted it laughingly, she said that she had been going to Mass lately with her Tía Gloria and her two cousins only because she knew her Tía Gloria liked the idea of that, Mariposa going to church with them at least *sometimes*, her Tía Gloria was very kind, she was helping Mariposa, she was giving Mariposa a place to live, and while Mariposa said that her aunt didn't like the idea of Mariposa working on East Sixth Street, there at Club El Pájaro Verde, Mariposa knew that if she went to the ten o'clock Mass with her aunt tomorrow that would help to calm the woman's fears, though Mariposa also admitted that she usually half dozed through everything at the Mass, from the singing accompanied by guitar at the Mass to the fuzzy-cheeked young priest who looked like a mere schoolboy nervously delivering his studiously memorized sermon, Mariposa was always tired after being out late working on Saturday, but, true, her aunt

would maybe be somewhat assured if Mariposa went to
Mass, her aunt wouldn't think that Mariposa was bound
to get into trouble working on East Sixth Street, Mariposa told him still again that she had worked at the club
just a little over a month, she told him that it was only
temporary, she wanted to get another job, other work, of
course, and then something happened, he was listening
but maybe he wasn't listening, because his forefinger
had reached out to touch the tiny gold cross that hung
from the fine gold chain no thicker than string about her
neck, it was odd the way it happened, and they were
talking, laughing, he had already said that she should
get herself another one of the ten-dollar Tecates, and
she had already told him, OK, she would get one in a
minute when he was ready for another, too, the tip of
his thick finger now touched the cross that she had let
drop back to the hollow contours of her very fragile col-
larbone, quite visible, atop the ridiculous halter top with
those impossible flaps, she was bare right to her smallish breasts for which she probably never did really need
a bra, and she wasn't sure why he did that, Mariposa
really didn't know, but his finger was surprisingly cold,
icy, and it could have been that his finger was cold because his hand had just been gripping the beer and the
bottle itself was very cold even with the napkin wrapped

around the cylinder of it, and when he touched the
cross, the thin gold metal, pressing it slightly to her
throat as he did it, the cold seemed to be in the cross
itself, and it was almost as if he himself did it instinc-
tively, without thinking, he seemed serious and intense
suddenly, and it was as if, yes, she could feel the cold of
it coming from his finger and then through the metal
against her flesh, but maybe she couldn't, he had gray
eyes, his tanned skin was leathery and the eyes were
fringed with wrinkles, and with his beige check Western
shirt unbuttoned for a few of its pearl snaps, that hair
on his chest wasn't gray but silvery, even white, he was
possibly older than she had first thought, in his fifties
but most likely late fifties, and the finger seemed to lin-
ger there, and she had to admit that she had a bit of a
start, a tinge of jumpiness, with his finger still there like
that, and then she lowered her eyes and looked down
over her nose again to the cross and his finger on it, and
he maybe noticed that she was doing so, and he slowly
removed the finger, as if he had been caught in something but making it look as if he wasn't alarmed about it,
he did it very slowly, smiling again, more like he had
been before, not looking as intense and serious, his gray
eyes, and with his hair cut short that way, Mariposa
thought again, you would have guessed that he was an

ex-military man even if he hadn't told you he was, and
the fact that he flew helicopters seemed so right for
him, La canción de Mariposa, the scars, and he was
laughing again, as easily as that, she wasn't jumpy anymore, as easily as that, and she wondered why she had
been jumpy when he had touched her there, she had
been putting her hand on the thigh of his jeans to make
a point now and then in the conversation, she had
showed him the cross, and then he had touched the
cross, it was as simple as that, nothing more, and he
said something about it now, tried to explain himself, or
he said, "I think it's damn good that you're Catholic,
darlin'," and then he corrected that, "But maybe I
shouldn't say damn when talking about religion, you being a Catholic, or how did you say it, the word for Catholic?," and she understood that, she told him "Católico,"
and then she said more emphatically, "Soy católica," she
nodded, and she liked this Anglo named Bill, she liked
the way he listened to her, asked her to say things as if
he wanted to hear them, as if he wanted to learn Spanish as much as she wanted, and wanted so very much,
to learn English, she needed better English, they talked
some more, and Mariposa, sitting at the counter along
the wall with him, beyond the end of the bar, she could
still see across the little half wall of cinderblocks paint-

ed glossily emerald green and to the other side and the dance floor there, she could see Espíritu standing at the turntable with his head encased in the headphones, probably lost in his general planning strategy, totally taken up by his work, adjusting the little buttons some on the black panel with its low-flashing signals to get everything exactly right, sliding a control up, sliding another down, looking at his other discs and old-fashioned tapes, studying them, choosing with considerable thought and great seriousness what to play next, and there were two major events that probably happened on any Saturday night in Club El Pájaro Verde, you could almost set your watch to them, Mariposa knew, but they hadn't happened yet, Mariposa went off to get the man another beer and herself another little ten-dollar Tecate, and . . .

(. . . and there was a sort of symmetry to the pair of events, because right when the bar would get most crowded on a Saturday night, when the music was loudest and the smoke was thickest, it seemed, first the gang boys would show with the one girl, a beautiful teenage

girl, sixteen, maybe seventeen, no more than that, the
gang boys materialized in a pack for their usual brief appearance, everybody knew how this worked, Fat Tommy
stepped aside at the door, he didn't wave them in but he
did nod to them, without smiling, and Fat Tommy in the
dark blue security guard uniform that showed his white
socks below the too-short pants, the shirt that didn't
button right across his wide front, he probably knew
more than anybody else how this worked, and for the
gang boys it wasn't a matter of coming to El Pájaro
Verde to drink or coming to have anything whatsoever to
do with the men who sat at the tables and shuffled to
and from the dance floor with the available B-girls, it
was more how the gang boys probably wanted to assert
their presence in this pocket of East Sixth Street, they
came in, a half-dozen of the boys and the one girl, and
the boys all wore calf-length baggy shorts that seemed
to be falling off, shedding from their bodies, their Satur-
day-night dress was nearly a caricature of rap attire, they
maybe wore oversize American sports-team jerseys with
giant medallions on giant chains and they always wore
expensive basketball shoes, what might have cost a good
portion of a week's wages for any of the other men
drinking here, complicated shoes with all that leather
and all that bright flashy trim like some exercise in fu-

turistic art gone wrong and the soles themselves on
some of those shoes that always intrigued Mariposa,
and when she had first seen those shoes she had found
herself staring at them, there was a thick layer of clear,
gummily soft plastic in between the sole itself and the
shoe, and encased in the clear plastic were rows of little
springy rubber coils, separating the two, like some kind
of suspension on some kind of a customized low-rider
car, they were crazy shoes, and the boys' heads were
buzz-cut so that you could see the skin underneath and
also any bump on the head or any ugly ripple at the
back of the neck, which is what they probably wanted
you to see, they didn't want to look like everybody else,
though the one gang boy who seemed to be with the girl
was different from the rest and, yes, he had on the same
baggy shorts that flopped like sails as he walked and he
had on the same type of very complicated expensive
basketball shoes, but he wasn't wearing a football or
baseball shirt and he himself didn't have any big medallion, like the medallion made from an expensive luxury
car's hood ornament that one boy with dark bushy eyebrows wore, or the heavy oblong medallion, cheaply
plated and showing what seemed to be a cartoon image
of a pile of gold bullion bars on the thick slab of it, that
another boy, very short and very stocky, wore, and this

particular gang boy wore no sunglasses hiding his eyes either, as some of them did, he was skinny and had light brown hair so he looked like an Anglo while he wasn't actually an Anglo, he wore a rap cap, sky blue, sideways, one of those flat-bill rap caps that, like the complicated basketball shoes, you had to study some to figure out, or Mariposa did, anyway, and if it seemed a little mystery how there was that clear space with invisibility like air itself in the soles of those shoes that caused you to look twice, then there was a little mystery in how sometimes those rap caps could be so big and almost float atop the head they were perched on the way they did, and there was a plastic headband inside, Mariposa eventually learned, it was actually the size of the head and kept the bigger cap anchored while that cap itself was attached to the band but held out from it, to let the cap appear to be nearly hovering like a halo, sort of suspended, this boy wore a droopy white undershirt, the sleeveless kind, with his baggy shorts, the cap was set not only sideways but at a sloping angle, too, very sky blue, the whole look of this one gang boy was, in fact, enough to make you wonder, the oddity of him being not very brown and with such light hair and looking like an Anglo even if he was Latino, all of that as accompanied by the rap cap and even the tattoos on both sides of his fair forearms, which Mariposa knew was where boys in this gang had their tattoos, where they showed the cryptic markings like something out of a horror movie in crude, smeared blue-black designs, dull, never any red, popped forever into their flesh with a buzzing ink-dribbling electric needle, the markings that pledged their affiliation, even their bravery and outright flaunting of death itself, and this was the boy that the girl was with, and it didn't mean that he was the leader and it didn't mean that because he was different for a Latino that he had this girl, he simply did have this girl, this beautiful, beautiful sixteen- or seventeen-year-old Latina girl, whose presence could sometimes bring the whole place to silence for a minute or two when she appeared in the midst of, overall, the shabby and worn and very grimy scene, the broken-downness of Club El Pájaro Verde, it was something you weren't sure of at all, seeing her in this run-down club, she didn't seem like she belonged here and in a way it didn't seem that she, in her flawless youth, did belong anywhere, she was something imagined just like so much else in Club El Pájaro Verde was all something imagined for Mariposa, the dream of it, and tonight the girl wore a skirt that wasn't only short but almost wasn't a skirt whatsoever, it was merely a black horizontal stripe that started somewhere well below her

navel and did what it had to do for a few tentative inch-
es to cover the tops of her slim teenager's thighs, nothing more, so that any man seeing her would stare at
what *pretended* to be a skirt, skimpy like that, and from
behind you could see below it, peeking out, the crescents of her bottom, and from the front you were almost
sure you could see a little satiny red triangular patch of
thong panties, X-marks-the-spot for the men, even if
you couldn't see that and even if her panties weren't red
thong panties, that's what a man might picture, or definitely would picture, she had long mahogany hair and
very high cheekbones and very full lips, her complexion
was flawless, she wore gold strappy high heels that
might have been from Payless but on her looked anything but that, they looked near magical, gold shoes
from some fairy tale, and her loose, sheer white long-
sleeve blouse was gauzily translucent so that you could
see the outline of the ringed tips of her small pert
breasts, snubbed, so that you could see the flesh of her
shoulders and arms, and you knew that with her being
with these gang boys it was beyond a simple miracle
that she herself didn't have some kind of a tattoo an-
nouncing her as their property, some kind of crude
marking, though there was something so ethereal and
almost otherworldly about her that anybody might in-

stinctively, and immediately, step in front of her if somebody ever did come near her with a buzzing needle, a
tattooer, to ward the guy off and defend her and tell him
to get the hell away, don't mar this innocence, this pris-
tine teenager, but her eyes were sleepy, half closed, dark
doe eyes that constantly seemed to be on the brink of
fluttering shut completely though they were open, she
was obviously high on something, pretty stoned all the
time when she showed at the club, close to sleepwalking, it seemed, but beautifully sleepwalking, and the
gang boys would stand around at the front corner of the
bar for a while under the TV rigged high up there, they
would talk among themselves, one of them looking
above him now and then to pretend he was interested in
that TV with its sound off, tuned in to Univisión or Azteca América, until Espíritu the disc jockey who certainly had been watching them all the while from his
back corner in the opposite end of the place, he seemed
to know what to do and exactly the moment to do it,
and as a *norteño* number finished its last accordion
chops and then the wrap-up of a final snare-drum rattle,
there came, suddenly booming even louder, resonating
like the first peal of thunder that you hear from a storm
when an exploding silver lightning bolt cracks in two the
shell of an enormous purple sky, yes, the thumping bass

line of a Mexican rap song, and otherwise there was no
Mexican rap ever played at Club El Pájaro Verde, Mariposa knew, that kind of music was for the big glitzy new
nightclubs with huge parking lots of asphalt as smooth
as black velvet and huge dance floors for the young, hip
Latinos, she had heard stories of those clubs, clubs
maybe on Riverside Drive south of the downtown in
Austin, she wasn't sure, there they would play rap and
reggaetón, a lot of music like Calle Trece's, and now
with that beat of the song his cue, the fair-haired gang
boy with his sideways rap cap started out from the bar
to the dance floor on the other side of the low emerald-
green cinderblock wall, nobody else was on the little
patch of worn marbleized black linoleum there, he did it
with no expression and no talk whatsoever, unimpressed
by anything around him, skinny, and he led behind him
the girl who was dressed so well that it was all too evi-
dent that she shouldn't be here and that she should be
at one of those big dance clubs on Riverside that supposedly were luxurious, expensive, that supposedly had
all sorts of different levels and showy chrome staircases
connecting the levels and endless deep, darkened, comfortably upholstered booths, she had a certain classi-
ness, thoroughly high or not, and here at Club El Pájaro
Verde the pulsating lights above the dance floor dropped

little red circles slow-bouncing like fallen balloons
across the linoleum, the speakers probably had a tough
time not ripping apart to just so many black shreds with
such gigantic, repeated, exploding slow bass, and the
two began to dance, nobody else on the floor, or she began to slowly, somnambulistically dance as she always
did, because the boy more or less just stood there, moving a little to the beat, shifting from one basketball shoe
to another, slow, looking around some but not looking at
her, while the teenage girl with him began, eyes half
closed, she gyrated, undulated around him slowly, moving her slim hips in that next-to-nothing skirt in a
churning motion, passing her flattened palms, caress-
ingly, over the sides of the sheer blouse and down onto
the sides of the skirt, almost some kinky video se-
quence, close to a strip-club routine, she would occasionally drape herself onto him, hang on his shoulder
some and keep dancing so very slow, and he might once
or twice casually glance at her, as if to say, "What the
hell are you doing now?," condescendingly, seemingly
completely uninterested, the sky-blue cap set sideways
on his head, he would then simply look around the club
again, she might move back a bit, facing him, and slowly
push both hands in a raking shove through the full
mane of mahogany hair, tilt her head back so the hair

spilled in a sheet as if in a shampoo ad, that mane of a
teenager's mahogany hair must have weighed a couple
of pounds, easily, she was still slowly churning, she
might move up behind him and churn with her hands
planted on her hips or planted on her behind while
making herself a spoon against him, the flat of the miniature skirt and surely what was there underneath the
skirt up against his baggy shorts like that, but even then
he wouldn't turn around, he would let her continue
moving to the thump-thumping of the repetitive bass
and the flow of the jerky, impromptu near-poetry of
rhyming syllables spoken gruffly that were the lyrics of
the rap, definitely L.A. Mexican rap, most all of the really good Mexican rap and hip-hop came out of L.A.,
Chicano rap, and if he did anything more than keep
standing there it was only to let one dangling hand
reach back to touch her behind him if she started the
spoon thing again at his back, to finally give her presence some acknowledgment but not too much, nonchalantly let her know that he knew she was there but never turning his head to look at her, he was cooler than
cool, and toward the end of the song she got even more
daring, she gyrated slow in front of him again, the mossy
eyelids shut now, her moist lips mechanically though
maybe silently uttering the lyrics along with the rapper,

she was obviously somewhere else, somewhere a million
miles away, being so high, so very, very high, and that
was the wind-up to the performance, the repeated raking with both of her hands through her hair again, back
from her forehead, slow, then lowering herself, lower
and lower, still gyrating her behind, showing beyond any
doubt the twin crescents now certainly peeking out
from under the black skirt when she squatted very low
like that, her exposed flesh, so maybe she did wear a
thong, or even nothing underneath, her bottom nearly
touching the scuffed-up linoleum of Club El Pájaro
Verde dusty with footsteps from all the dancing that
night, she was a little wobbly on the beautiful gold
strappy high heels, then she slowly rose up again in
front of him, reversing it all, so after corkscrewing herself down she was now corkscrewing herself up, higher
and higher, and atop the spikes of the high heels her ankles were like tiny, delicate nuts, the gold straps of the
shoes crisscrossing up around her calves, the little rib-
bon ties were bowed in front, beautiful, beautiful shoes,
she slowly raised herself, gyrating as her pouty lips scan-
ningly brushed up along his body, past the baggy shorts
and past his hard, flat stomach and past his bony chest
in the cheap undershirt he wore, until she was standing
again with her head snuggling sleepily into his neck, like

a puppy, draped on him, but slowly moving to the
rhythm all the while, and the gang boy only looked from
side to side, as if he still wasn't as much as tempted to
be vaguely interested now, and while the whole routine
of it might have been the stuff of a topless bar, as said,
some intricate table dance routine, here it was really
anything but that, here it was the odd purity of this
beautiful girl at sixteen or seventeen, breathtaking, it
was the youth of her perfect body unsullied by all the
dirt and weariness of East Austin and El Pájaro Verde,
and that was what made this first, near regular event of
a Saturday night part of the symmetry, one end of perhaps the entire arc of life, because after she left, after
the gang boys just strolled out as casually as they had
strolled in, a film in reverse development, stony-faced
Fat Tommy nodding to them, there came next a couple
of songs from Espíritu to try to get a few people dancing
again, but after the appearance of the ethereal teenage
girl in the first fragile blossom of being sixteen or seventeen, what all the B-girls themselves could only be rather stunned by, Club El Pájaro Verde needed some adjusting, nobody wanted to dance yet, and it was as if Espíritu understood that, though he probably didn't understand it, but nevertheless, and maybe more out of in-
stinct than anything else, he did what he always did on

other Saturday nights at Club El Pájaro Verde after that performance, and probably he did fully realize, in simplest terms, that he really needed to change the mood, restore normalcy, and so came that other end of the arc, completing the symmetry, because at Club El Pájaro Verde there could be the *viejos* who just wandered in from the street, specifically two old stubbled men who could have been from a different interpretation of life altogether, *borrachos*, drunks, obviously homeless, who maybe had long before made the arduous journey themselves up from whatever village where they had once lived deep in Mexico, a village near lost Zacatecas or lost Aguascalientes or somewhere in the very lost Estado de Chiapas almost clear down to Guatemala that didn't even have a town of reasonable size like Zacatecas or Aguascalientes for a village to be close to, identified with, they maybe had once come north, years ago, hopeful and determined, and they had worked hard, they maybe had once had wives and children to whom they regularly sent money back, they might have worked construction, which it often seemed everybody did, or they might have been taken on in a kitchen doing prep for a restaurant or hired in a muffler or tire shop, sweating through twelve-hour days and not daring to ask for overtime, their faces grease-smeared and knuckles thoroughly bloodied from the angular tools, until, after too many years, they got older and just didn't remember Mexico anymore, until they didn't have any real job anymore, and by then they didn't think about their families left behind anymore, it was all forgotten, altogether too many years had passed, so the question of who had documentation papers or who didn't have the documentation papers wasn't even a dimly recalled issue to them anymore, they were beyond that, outside of it, somehow they were at last free the way that everybody who came across the border always longed to be, if honest, they didn't care much about money now, they were old, *viejos*, granting they probably weren't *that* old, and this particular pair, yes, both stubble-faced, one in his old-fashioned conical straw *sombrero*, like a *campesino*, and the other with a marked limp, they did manage to scrounge up enough change to come in and buy a beer or two, and of course they were even beyond getting any work as day laborers, when the local contractors and farmers showed in gleaming new pick-up trucks at the currently very popular congregating spot at a boarded-up warehouse downtown, and all but toothless, drunk most of the time, yes, with their being so broken, nobody as much as thought of hiring the likes of them even as day laborers anymore, lowly *jornaleros*, nobody wanted them

even when they slept on the platforms at that ramshackle warehouse, a place the wise-guy city cops sarcastically referred to as the "Downtown Job Fair," the *viejos*
camping out there all night, to be hung-over but ready
in the foggy dawn, standing around with the other men
and waiting for the first pick-up trucks to arrive looking
for cheap labor, nobody was going to hire them for anything, not everyday landscaping chores, not even the no-
toriously back-breaking dawn-to-dusk farm and ranch
work outside of Austin, like picking pecans or peaches
out in the Hill Country, they were old, foul-breathed,
thoroughly drunk most of the time, drifting about the
city, occasionally attempting some panhandling, trying
that ruse where you stood in the heat and held up a
hand-lettered corrugated cardboard sign at a stoplight
along an access road beside I-35 or slowly walked between the lanes of the stopped traffic there during rush
hour with a held-out styrofoam cup, as drivers made
sure they rolled up their windows fast for protection before somebody *like that* got within two cars of them, the
drivers nervously waiting, possibly praying, for the light
to change, and now the *viejos* didn't care, it seemed,
they didn't care how they looked or what they did as
long as they could get enough money, somehow, in some
way, for repeated quart bottles of beer from a conve-

nience store to keep them drunk, they lived on the
street, slept behind buildings or in littered lots and got
occasional meals from charity organization hand-out
trucks, they used the bathrooms in fast-food restaurants
and clubs like El Pájaro Verde and would always *make
sure* that they saved enough of their change to buy a
beer or two on Saturday night from what they had
cadged around town, which entitled them to the privi-
lege of using the bathrooms, cleaning up some in there,
yet despite all that they always seemed to be entirely
happy, noisier than the quiet younger men, they probably were also entirely crazy, if truth be known, the old
men were *locos*, Mariposa had heard everybody say they
were, and what Espíritu did this Saturday night was
what he did on other Saturday nights to keep the flow
going there in the club, he had done it more than once
before, that was his responsibility, he dictated the tem-
po, and after the event of the beautiful teenage girl
dancing slowly and mesmerizingly that way, there would
come this second event involving the *locos*, and to pick
things up Espíritu would put on the number that everybody called, generically and half in English, "The Cerveza Song," the tooting tuba and the loopy lyrics boun-
cily talking about "Cerveza! Quiero cerveza!" and the
rest of it, the lyrics dumbly repeating the line about lik-

ing *cerveza* over and over, liking *cerveza* at the seaside, liking *cerveza* in the mountains, liking *cerveza* while riding in a car, just *liking cerveza*, and the stubble-faced *locos*, the limping one and the one recently having taken to wearing the farmer's *sombrero* made of rough basket-woven grass, fraying, they danced with each other, flapping their arms like chicken wings, looking at their feet in worn boots that were doing a step that didn't seem Mexican whatsoever even if it was akin to the classic hat dance, theirs was more of a jig, toothlessly shouting about *Cerveza!* along with the lyrics, the pair of them laughing, cackling like chickens as well, people watching them dancing alone out there on the floor laughed, but for Mariposa they, too, were part of the dream even if she couldn't have expressed it that way, because this was the other end of the spectrum, even if she couldn't have expressed that either, these were two forgotten old men who should have already been dead, and, in fact, they could have been dead, they could have been a pair of rattling skeletons dancing together, and there was that symmetry of them going out there after the beautiful teenage girl had given her performance, it was what told the whole story, beauty and ugliness, ugliness and beauty, youth and age, age and youth, but not *just* that, something else, too, that you couldn't ever name, a

blank, black, bottomless void that seemed to say again
that perhaps none of any of it mattered, nothing mattered, really, all was beyond futile, meaningless, and before long everybody was noisy again, on the very next
song the B-girls were busy again and taxi-dancing with
the men as usual, talking at the tables, delivering more
beers, and, true, energetically hustling . . . and . . .)

. . . and Mariposa was talking to the Anglo, she
didn't as much as pay any real attention to those two
"events" this Saturday night, in fact, she was so caught
up with talking to the Anglo, she probably didn't even
notice the wandering vendors who came in and strolled
aimlessly about with their flowers and inevitable chew-
ing gum and packages of too-sweet candy displayed in
the hoop-handle metal trays they carried, she maybe
looked around once in a while to see if tall Ignacio in
his fine black Western clothes had shown up, old-
fashionedly polite Ignacio from Durango, it was well after ten, he probably wouldn't show, after all, if he hadn't
shown yet, he usually came at ten on the dot, and Mariposa talked to the Anglo, both of them with the second

round of drinks he had bought, or second for her and now third for him, and it must have been in the course of those two regular Saturday night events happening out on the dance floor that she had started emphasizing to him how her working at the club like this was only temporary, she didn't want to have to resort to working at a fast-food place again, she *definitely* didn't want that, she needed to learn to speak English better, La canción de Mariposa, she told him more about Honduras, she told him that she had almost finished the courses for the degree at the technical high school in her town but the larger problem was that there wasn't much work in her town, it had grown in size, many people didn't work, and what work there was involved just the two things that seemed to be the only work that there was any-where in Honduras, either on the plantations with their packing plants for bananas and coffee and pineapples or in the huge new factories that manufactured clothing, those weren't good jobs, they paid next to nothing and with such work you never got anywhere, she had attend-ed technical high school and was trained for something much better, her brother had offered to help her, he had gone to Tennessee years before, much older than her so she really didn't know him that well, Mariposa was tell-ing the Anglo a lot of things, La canción de Mariposa, her brother had been able to get her the job at the big computer-supply store called Completely Wired because his boss seemed to like the idea of her brother having said that his sister had gone to a technical high school, but as it turned out she really had to have better English, and she was cold in Tennessee, cold all the time, it snowed, then she worked the awful job at the Burger King in Tennessee, "It sounds like you've gotten around some, darlin', done some traveling, now haven't you," this Anglo Bill said, listening to her, smiling, she liked him, he flew choppers, and she said that, in truth, she really couldn't take much more of working at Club El Pájaro Verde now, she realized that she might not be ready yet for a good job in the States but there were other jobs she should have taken, or at least she should have looked for, and she said that she really needed to learn English better, if she had better English she could maybe do what Fat Tommy was doing, take some classes, "Fat Tommy?" the Anglo asked her, and she told him that Fat Tommy was over there, the bouncer and security guard, the Anglo named Bill looked toward the door and saw him, Mariposa and the Anglo did communicate pretty well, usually found the words to say what they meant, but she didn't tell him all of it, how there was that once she had talked with Fat Tommy when she ran

into him at the laundromat on Chicón Street and she
was doing the wash for her aunt, the only time she had
really spoken to Fat Tommy outside of the club, she was
surprised to see him there that afternoon, and she had
always just thought, or assumed, that Fat Tommy lived
farther up on the East Side of Austin, there around
Eleventh and Twelfth Streets, which were the black
neighborhoods with barbecue places and hair salons
and nightclubs for blacks and also the many little makeshift churches, where, passing them, you sometimes
thought you could feel the buildings wildly shaking as
the charged choirs practiced within, tiny wooden
churches or tiny cinderblock churches, who knows how
many churches, with plastic-lettered signs out front telling the pastor's name as well as that particular week's
Bible message, but Fat Tommy did speak Spanish, he
was what they called African American though maybe
he did have one parent who was Dominican or even
Panamanian, or maybe he had just grown up a few
streets lower down here on the East Side where the
city's old black neighborhoods, rickety, metamorphosed
into the city's old Mexican neighborhoods, rickety, Mariposa would never know how he had learned Spanish,
but when she did see Fat Tommy at the laundromat that
day it was good to run into him, the yellow washers and

dryers thumped, people around them sorted and folded, there was the clean, pure smell of detergent mixed with the fresh heat of the dryers themselves, and that was good, and at first Fat Tommy didn't say much to her, he was like that, very quiet, he was sitting there with a big textbook on a yellow plastic scoop chair in the row of them and squeakily underlining things he read with a green highlighter, and he said, lowly, "Hola," and she said the same to him, "Hola," there was no talk about the club, what they had in common, it was as if it was something they shared, but away from the club Fat Tommy didn't want to talk about it, and away from Club El Pájaro Verde Mariposa surely didn't want to talk about it, she heaped the plastic basket with the clothes to be washed for her aunt and cousins up onto the bare masonite table, she started loading the clothes and counting out the quarters, carefully measuring the Purex detergent her aunt always bought at the dollar store, and then she sat with Fat Tommy, who folded the book shut and left the green highlighter inside it as a marker, and in his hands, which themselves were fat, the book, even being as big as it was and a textbook, looked too small for him, as if it wasn't Fat Tommy there in khakis and a fresh cotton T-shirt but, yes, a bear performing a circus trick of reading a book, which was when he told her that he was taking courses at ACC, he explained it was Austin Community College, and he told her that he wasn't officially enrolled for any degree and as for now he was just taking courses, she wasn't sure she followed all of it but he seemed to explain that he hadn't graduated from high school, he had gotten close, he had even completed the required twelve grades of school, but they made you take a test in Texas to graduate, it wasn't easy, or the math part wasn't at all easy for him, a state test, and he failed it twice, Fat Tommy's voice was soft, slow, he said that the same thing always happened to a lot of boys like him who played American football, they played for the team at Johnston High and never got a diploma, because that was his school, Johnston, and he told her that it sometimes got confused with another Austin school, LBJ, which was Lyndon B. Johnson High, Fat Tommy received no diploma, but now, a few years later, he had taken what he explained to her in Spanish was an equivalency test, he passed it, including the math, he was taking some courses now that would allow him to officially get into a program for a certificate in medical services, he wanted to work at a hospital, but first there were basic courses almost like high school courses that he needed before he could enter the program, he said that the book he was studying was a World History one, and he showed her the cover of the thing, where it said *Our Many Pasts* and with a checker board of bright-colored tourist-shot photos of the ruins in maybe ancient Greece and landmarks in Europe, like the Eiffel Tower and Big Ben, also street scenes in modern cities in other places still, maybe a place like Hong Kong in Asia and maybe a place like Lagos in Africa and maybe a place like Mexico City itself, though Mariposa certainly couldn't identify the cities depicted, or she couldn't do so as accurately as that, but she liked the pictures on the book's cover, Fat Tommy opened the book to where the green highlighter split its pile of pages and he showed her what he had been reading, studying for this week's class, a chapter early on, not about ancient Greece but about the Roman Empire, there was a map representing how very far that Empire had once stretched, with fine print inside the caption balloons noting the period of settlement in various regions and the exact years, B.C. or A.D., he showed her the illustration on the opposite page, an inserted oil-painting scene of a gladiator facing golden lions in the crowded Roman Colosseum, a long spear in one upraised hand and the large beasts in a semicircle staring at him, Fat Tommy said that it wasn't just something that got made up for

the movies, he had been reading about it, that happened, men fighting lions in the Colosseum, he said
that it was a very good course, this course about *Our
Many Pasts*, he said that she might want to take a class
or two at ACC where it wasn't like high school, and at
ACC it wasn't a matter of the teachers having to be
more like policemen than anything else, ACC was different, he had a good teacher for this course, and Mariposa said that she needed better English, it was the first
thing she had to do, learn to speak English better, and
she had noticed when he had opened up the book that
there was a full-color map of the world today on the inside endpapers, one hemisphere in the front and the
other in the back, she told him that she wanted to show
him something, she leaned over as she sat beside him
and flopped the book's pages to the front endpapers, the
Western Hemisphere, she pointed out to him where
Honduras was, she showed him the orange lump of it, a
small jig-saw puzzle piece, in between Guatemala and
Nicaragua, she had come all the way from there, she
told him, Fat Tommy looked at it seriously, studying the
map, he admitted that he sometimes got confused with
those countries in Central America, exactly where each
of them was in relation to the others, but he liked learning now exactly where Honduras was, and he liked the

way that there were two oceans even for a place as small
as that dark-orange puzzle piece of Mariposa's Honduras, and, actually, he seemed as quietly amazed by that
fact as he had been by the picture of the snarling golden
lions on the sands of the cavernous amphitheater in ancient Rome, he half wondrously repeated that it was
very interesting, the way her country had two oceans,
the Atlantic Ocean and the Pacific Ocean, Fat Tommy
told her all of that in his slow way, still staring at the
map, obviously thinking more about it, possibly still
amazed, or impressed, that such a small country could
actually have coasts on two such large, very important
oceans, and she admitted to him that living in the
mountains she had seen neither, but she said that she
thought he was right, the Caribbean was part of the Atlantic Ocean so it did mean two *oceans* for Honduras,
he said in his Spanish that there are so many amazing
things to know about the world, so many amazing things
to learn, she liked Fat Tommy, and of course she didn't
tell the Anglo named Bill that entire story of finding Fat
Tommy in the laundromat one day, but she maybe
thought of it, flashed to it, Mariposa, but she did tell the
Anglo about ACC, and she said that she wanted to take
courses there herself someday, she said that what she
really knew now was that she needed the kind of work

that would allow her to take courses and also to learn more English, and she said that she had been given some advice by her Tía Gloria's friend who lived in Dove Springs, there with her kids and a husband who worked on a house-painting crew, Mariposa told the Anglo that she helped take care of the woman's kids sometimes, and the woman, Teresa, had told Mariposa that the best kind of work for somebody like her would be cleaning houses, that was good work and it allowed you to arrange for flexible hours, the woman had said that if you did the work well for one person, showed you were conscientious and reliable, they would recommend you to another, "Limpiar," Mariposa told him, but he didn't seem to understand, she smiled, it was fun trying to find the right word, as *limpiar* became what she said next, "Limpiadora," then "Limpiadora de casas," a cleaner of houses, and with that he finally did understand, she was touching his jeans at the knee again as they sat there talking, an automatic response from her when she realized that he understood what she meant, and in the course of the talk she maybe noticed him looking not right at her sometimes but looking down and below her face, though he wasn't looking at her smallish breasts there, visible beneath the lime-green halter top that she had been so self-conscious about all night, that she never could get to lay right on her skinny torso, she never could or never would be able to knot that bow in front *exactly* right, and she saw that it was happening again, he was looking not into her hazel eyes that he had already complimented her on, they were indeed almost amber, he was looking at something else, lower down, he was looking again at the tiny cross lying there in nest of her neck bones, staring at it again, and for Mariposa it was like before, when he had touched it, what had made her a little jumpy, but maybe it wasn't like that, because he looked up now and smiled when he realized that she had noticed him looking, she maybe liked the fact that he liked the cross, that he liked that she was *católica*, and she told him more about the kind of work she wanted, that it wasn't to be confused with working as a maid or a cleaning lady at a hotel or motel, those jobs weren't good, but if you had houses to clean in the right neighborhoods, well, that was good, and that's when it started, because then it did start, but she didn't know that it had started, *La canción de Mariposa, the scars, the Anglo sitting there listening to her,* he told her that she really should think of something better than that, better than cleaning houses, "a pretty little thing like you," he said, but she told him that, no, she had thought a lot about it, explained it all again to him, she

needed flexible hours, the flexible hours would allow
her to take classes, she wouldn't be tired all day from
working late either, and with him saying "Cómo se dice"
who knows how many times more, he eventually told
her that he understood, he said that actually it was good
that she had a plan, "Not only a pretty little thing, darlin', but you're a smart little thing, too," and she said
that anything was better than staying here working as a
B-girl at Club El Pájaro Verde, or anything but going to
work in a fast-food place, because the time she had
worked in Burger King in Nashville had surely taught
her that, she didn't want to think about Nashville, she
most of all didn't want to think about working in the
Burger King in Nashville, *La canción de Mariposa, the
scars, the Anglo, La canción de Mariposa*, it had been terrible in Nashville, she said, the Anglo named Bill nodded, it had been *very* terrible in Nashville, she said, and
then it happened, at last it *really* happened, because she
had never shown anybody in Club El Pájaro Verde the
scars before, and, no, she hadn't shown him the scars at
first, it was only now, after they had been talking for a
while, or they seemed to have been talking forever, and
one minute she was simply talking, telling him more
things, the two of them trying to find the words, still
laughing now and then, both of them, and the next min-

ute she was telling him everything about Nashville, very serious, she could never again work in any fast-food place, Taco Bell or McDonald's or Burger King, nothing had been worse in her entire life than the job at the Burger King in Nashville, and that's when she did it, that's when she put down her little red can of Tecate again, placed it on the shelf behind her, it was after the beautiful teenage girl had left with the gang boys, after the clowning old men, *locos*, had given up on their silly dancing, Mariposa first tightened again the halter top's two lime-green flaps, untied the bow then retied the whole thing in front before she spoke, and then, more childish than ever, somehow more pleading than ever, more in need of something she couldn't name but that possibly she was just trying very hard to believe in, and so much of everything there in Club El Pájaro Verde was but a dream lately, she slowly lifted both her thin bare arms before her, palms down, suddenly hoping she wouldn't cry, she turned her hands over side by side so he could see the ugly scars, red and deeply rippled like piled satin at the base of her palms, so ugly, spreading onto her wrists, no, you wouldn't notice the scars at first but with her forearms turned over like that and even in the low light of the club they appeared to be very severe, painful just to view, she spoke the best she could in her broken English, she told him how that working at the Burger King you sometimes had to grab for the handle of the deep-fryer basket with both hands, they were big and very heavy square baskets, how you wore dirty white fireproof mitts to do it, but sometimes you didn't get them on right, or they slipped off some, the mitts were bulky, loose, and you had to move fast when the timer's beep sounded, you always had to move so fast because her manager always wanted the fries cooked exactly right, it didn't happen to her just once, it happened repeatedly, such a basket's handle could be like a red-hot fireplace poker if you grabbed it wrong, the scalding oil splashing up, the hurt of it, the burns and the blistering and the scars, more of them, compounding day after day and aching, the burns healing some, oozingly crusting over, but then getting just that much worse when she got burned again before the layering of previous burns had even had a chance to start to heal, which is what had happened to her, but she didn't complain, you couldn't complain, they would fire you in a minute because they knew that you couldn't complain, back then she was still feeling somewhat guilty about having lost the job at Completely Wired, she said, she had disappointed her brother, and she was also very much illegal, totally *indocumentada*, yes, Mariposa

showed him the scars, the scars that she had never
shown to anybody else in El Pájaro Verde, and that was
when he took one of her hands in his own large and
leathery hand, she looked at him, he wasn't that young
at all, if he was in his fifties it was unquestionably late
fifties, as she had suspected before, the gray hair, the
lines not only around his eyes but deep in his long
cheeks, his teeth looked somehow old, yellowish, not
very white, and he held one of her hands as if it was
something he was carefully examining, then he used his
other hand to pass the blunt tips of the fingers over the
scars, he kept doing that, lightly petting them, over and
over and over again, feeling the ridges of them, up and
down, slowly and almost hungrily memorizing the wavy
lines of them, the uneven lumps of them, as if he was
going to be tested on the look of them, as if he thought
they were beautiful, and close to her like that his breath
was beery, damp, he petted the scars, *which was when
she got scared, very scared, not just jumpy but scared,
there was something not right about the way he kept petting the scars, kept looking at them, it was worse than
when he had touched the little cross, it made Mariposa
dizzy, until he did finally drop her hand from the two of
his, her hand that fell limp like a shed petal,* and now he
looked at his watch, a giant chrome-plated watch, actu-

ally, with a black face and a number of smaller dials, a man who flew helicopters would have a watch like that, she thought, he smiled, and then she didn't feel scared, she liked this Anglo named Bill, and while her eyes, the eyes that everybody told her were so very rare, while her eyes had glassed up some when she talked of Nashville, while she had been on the brink of tears then, wanting to simply cry and cry, unabashedly and at last, she hadn't cried when she showed the scars to him, she managed not to, but she had wanted so much to cry, cry about the scars, cry about *everything*, she straightened her back a bit now, he looked at the giant complicated watch again, he said that he had to get going, it was nearly eleven, he explained to her that three Budweisers was his personal limit when he was working for a client and flying, the regulations for pilots were tough on that sort of thing, no alcohol after midnight, and he was flying tomorrow, he was in Austin to use a rental helicopter to fly some developers who were viewing a large tract of land that they were considering buying out beyond the western edge of the city, he explained, and he said that he had taken them there once already earlier this day, Saturday, he was a little tired from all that flying, he said that they had brought him in because he knew how to fly the model of big helicopter they rented, what was needed for this job, and he explained that when developers like the bunch he had transported today were looking at land they just wanted to circle around and around, study it for a while, let everything sink in, it wasn't much fun, they wanted to get a good idea of the lay of that land before they invested their big money, and then he said something else, putting his finished Budweiser with the napkin around it down on the shelf-like counter, steadying the bottle a little, and at first it didn't sit right because the napkin, which overlapped the base, too, made it wobbly, and he said that while she had been talking "a little light bulb went off in this old stone noggin, darlin'," he said "darlin'" an awful lot, he said that he might just be able to help her get a start in what she had in mind, he said that he had already spent time with these developers, and through them he knew of other people in Austin as well, he had some good contacts, he said that the kind of people he knew probably could use somebody to help out with cleaning in their homes, somebody who was certainly reliable and conscientious and honest, and he would make a few calls in the morning about it, talk to some people, yes, he just might be able to help her (what the police in Albuquerque and Phoenix did have to go on, what they seemed to be putting together from the questioning of

other girls who somehow had managed not to go along
with what he suggested, was that he did have that way
about him, more than friendly, making himself seem
more than understanding, and the police had a descrip-
tion of him being older, but for a while that was disput-
ed, a lucky break for this man whose name was Edward
Pacek, and the truth of the matter was that the investi-
gation went in an entirely wrong direction for a while as
the police tried to work up a pattern to the crimes,
which had been unspeakable, they were *always* vicious,
there was *always* dismemberment, and in the case of
one young woman, a kindergarten teacher who had last
been seen alive in an all-night self-service car wash in
Phoenix, even if it wasn't very late at night when she
had last been seen there, only nine or so, in that case
the information gathered became confusing, two other
young women who had also used the car wash themselves the same night claimed they had encountered a
younger man in a red Chevrolet Camaro and he had
tried to talk to each of these other young women that
night, the police concentrated on the lead for months,
the police kept looking for a younger man, but the sug-
gestion of a suspicious older man was more frequent, it
had turned up repeatedly, and there was somebody using a story about flying helicopters and that had turned

up several times, it was definitely something to follow
up on, and while Edward Pacek had never as much as
been in the military, didn't know anything about flying
helicopters other than what you might pick up on a TV
show, or maybe watching the local evening news that
had an aerial traffic reporter, he had used the story before, he probably knew that it impressed girls, and, in
truth, Edward Pacek ran a discount furniture store in
Tucson, he had taken over its operation after his father
died years before, the store was on Oracle Road, he
lived alone in the same simple enough fifties tract house
in suburban Tucson where he had been raised by his
parents and that was eventually willed to him by his
widowed mother, Edward Pacek a lifelong bachelor now
in late middle age, and there were many young women
who had been questioned in connection with the
crimes, the police needed leads, there had been the
slaying of the seven young women so far who were his
victims in two states, and some of the women questioned told the police that they had talked to a man who
acted suspiciously, but this man said nothing about helicopters, the man they had talked to was pleasant, even a
lot of fun for a guy that age, probably in his fifties, they
said, he seemed to have a nice way about him, but this
man had told each of them that he was a cattle rancher

not a pilot, he said that he owned a large spread with well over twenty thousand acres, this man apparently had told several young women around Albuquerque exactly that, in fact, how his ranch was very large, another of Edward Pacek's stories, something else that he knew impressed girls, as the police started going through electronic files for anything they had on cattle ranchers with any criminal background that might suggest a connection, and that led nowhere, they looked for prosperous ranchers just as they had looked for area helicopter pilots, before they decided that it, too, entailed but a story, which is when the police again began looking into what they had been told by the two girls who had both given, adamantly and in detail, their own information when questioned, gone on about it, the strange young guy in his twenties, who one said had been wearing wraparound sunglasses at night and who the other said hadn't, they were questioned again and did agree that he was about twenty-five and he drove a souped-up red Chevrolet Camaro, they both claimed he had approached them, separately and an hour or so apart at the car wash in Phoenix the night when the young woman who was a victim there had last been seen alive, but that didn't develop into anything, and then there was a gap for a year or so, nothing seemed to connect,

no viable angle developing whatsoever, but the police
were still hoping to put it together, waiting for something, they realized all the crimes were similar, it would
require a special squad, they decided, where the two
states could work together even if no federal officers
had yet been brought into it, the FBI had hedged, said
they needed more substantial evidence that the crimes
involved a crossing of state lines, so the FBI wasn't involved, but the police finally got approval for a joint bi-
state squad with several officers in the two cities as-
signed at least part-time to it, a detective named Mac-
Lean in Albuquerque made it pretty much his personal
mission to launch the squad, he was determined to
move toward finding this guy when he saw the photos,
and after the third one of the crimes in Albuquerque,
the disappearance of the young woman last seen alive
when leaving at ten-thirty P.M. a chain drugstore where
she worked as a checkout, across from the rebuilt and
still handsome adobe Santa Fe Railroad station downtown, now Amtrak, after her brutal murder the police
there received a mailed packet containing black-and-
white photographs, large glossies, of dismembered body
parts, hacked apart and spread out on what seemed to
be flattened brown wrapping paper that actually might
have been cut from standard supermarket bags, the dis-

play having been photographed in a wooded area, fallen leaves and pine needles on the ground around the squares of paper, the killer was obviously taunting the Albuquerque police, and MacLean thought that at last he had something solid to go on, he got the two police departments, in Albuquerque and Phoenix, to pool together on all information they had, to communicate more and cooperate fully in trying to link the four crimes in Phoenix with the three in Albuquerque, this Detective Sergeant MacLean had the glossies examined in a state-of-the-art West Coast university lab, analyzed thoroughly by those top-notch L.A. forensic criminology experts, but he didn't need any expert analysis to tell him what his own basic deductive logic did tell him, he was certain that, if nothing else, the idea of a younger man was off, and what had been established at the very start, before talking to the girls at the car wash, was most likely the case, the police were dealing with an older man, MacLean was sure of it, and a younger man would have used digital photography, wouldn't be able to develop photographs like those himself, that type of dark-room photo processing was fast becoming a lost skill, and nobody would be crazy enough to have a local photomat or drugstore develop such pictures, the search, with lengthy questioning, was intensified and became a priority, for MacLean, anyway, who was working on it full-time now, since the formation of the squad a month before, it had turned very personal, he had two young kids himself, both daughters, and he wanted to get this guy, there were more interviews with more girls who might have encountered somebody older and suspicious near the scenes of the crimes, both in Albuquerque and Phoenix, the other possible crime scenes, too, though MacLean or anybody else couldn't have had any way of knowing that Edward Pacek was already aware that he should maybe go a little farther off to be safe, expand his territory, so to speak, until things settled down some, and from Tucson he could easily drive to Texas if he took a long weekend away from managing matters at the furniture store, the operation could get by without him for a few days, he knew, he had a reliable four-person sales staff, and he would use a rental car for anonymity in case anybody might be looking for his own navy-blue Toyota Camry sedan, he had heaped the nylon gym bag with the clanking implements he needed into the trunk before leaving Tucson, all of which is to say, the police still had only a scattering of vaguely workable leads to go on, not enough to create any truly solid profile, if they were entirely honest with themselves about it), and the Anglo named Bill told Mariposa now that one of the best things about her working in homes of good people and doing some cleaning and housekeeping like that, on her own and arranging for her own hours, would be that it would help her in what she kept telling him she needed, she could work on her English in those surroundings, or not even have to work on it in such a sensible situation, and she would get practice just by talking with people and their families while on the job, it would be solid, valuable experience, and he asked her if she had a pen, and she knew the word he said, "pen," a *pluma* it was, and she said, enthusiastic now, her teeth glistening when she smiled, she told him that of course she had "a *pen*," she wriggled her behind on the red plastic seat of the bar stool and with some maneuvering tugged the orange-and-white ballpoint from her jeans' front pocket, it advertised a local U-Haul franchise, Mariposa had no idea where she had gotten it and she must have picked it up at the bar, she held it up like a school kid showing something to the teacher, and he was already leaning across her to reach over to her brown plastic tray set atop the shelf and take a napkin from the few of them lying on the tray, he put the napkin flat on that little shelf along the wall and took the pen from her, he clicked it a couple of times and seemed to approve of

the look of it, indicating it would do just fine, he told
her that what they could do was get together the next
day, maybe for lunch, he would make some calls in the
morning to people who might know other people and
check around for her concerning the house-cleaning
work and then the two of them could talk about it,
Mariposa smiled as he spoke, and he explained that he
didn't have to meet the developers out at the small pri-
vate airport beside Austin's large Bergstrom International Airport until later in the afternoon, the two of them
could have lunch, he suggested it again, Mariposa said
"OK," and he made a joke out of that, too, saying he
wondered if "OK" was the most universal word of all,
what you probably could say to anybody who spoke any
other language and they would understand you, he
laughed, or she thought that was what he said about the
word "OK," her English wasn't very good at all, and he
told her that he was staying at a place called the Rodeway Inn on North I-35, he said that he didn't know the
phone number for the motel but he did know his room
number, 224, and all she had to do was look up the
name of the place, find it under "Motels" and in "los pá-
ginas amarillos," he said, raising his eyebrows inquisi-
tively as if to ask whether he had gotten that right, she
said "Sí," she nodded, she didn't correct him, tell him

that it should be *las* and *amarillas*, and he said it would
be easy to find the number, he began to write, he had a
big gold ring with a maroon stone on one finger, he said
that once she got through on the phone to the motel
desk she just had to give the number of the room, they
would connect her, and he continued to write the block-
ish letters, a man's coarse, rough printing and the ink
sinking into the sort of cushion of the soft napkin as he
marked out each line and each loop to methodically
form each letter (and while he was writing Mariposa did
look around the smoky club, and she saw Fat Tommy
still in the doorway, he seemed to be looking right at her
with the Anglo, and then, stranger, she saw Inés back at
the table with Carmen and the other girls, the table
with the Carta Blanca logo, a red oval, stamped in each
corner of its white porcelain top, but for some reason,
and *very* strangely, Inés wasn't talking to the other girls,
she wasn't plucking the silver cell phone from between
her breasts or she wasn't scanning the room herself to
see if any man needed a *copa*, she was sitting there, the
wing of black hair hiding one eye again, and she, too,
was looking right at Mariposa, watching her with the
Anglo who was writing something down on a napkin),
he finished what he was writing, he handed her the napkin, Mariposa looked, he had written BILL, RODEWAY

INN, I-35, ROOM 224, he said again that he had to fly later in the afternoon, Sunday, but if she called him they could meet somewhere, or he could drive over and pick her up in East Austin, she could name a spot, he said again that he liked this idea, he really thought he could help her, "A guy like me has to be good for something once in a while, now doesn't he, darlin'," he said that, and Mariposa folded the napkin very carefully, first in half then in quarters, she tucked the square of it in one of the embroidered back pockets of her jeans, and she assured him she would call, she would call right after Mass, she told him, she smiled, thanking him, and he winked, and then the Anglo left, and no sooner was he gone than she noticed that Ignacio had arrived, Ignacio was here in Club El Pájaro Verde, after all, along with his *compadres*, Mr. Álvarez was shaking their hands, as he sometimes did with regulars, and . . .

. . . and Mariposa did see Ignacio already looking around, she was sure he was looking around for her, and Inés and the other girls at that table didn't as much as attempt to approach the contingent, as Ignacio and the young men with him walked away from Mr. Álvarez in his light blue *guayabera*, Mr. Álvarez having warmly greeted them, Ignacio had on the black outfit, with a black shirt and black jeans and black boots, there was the large silver belt buckle and the black Stetson, he had a trim mustache, and after he headed with those other young men to the side of the club with the dance floor, the bunch of them took folding chairs from one table in the corner and placed them right beside the green-painted wooden railing, like a corral's fencing, along the front of the perfect square of the dance floor, the red light from above still pulsating, they would set up the chairs there to watch the entertainment and that was enough for them, the show of the other people dancing in the club, and when Mariposa approached them Ignacio nodded, lifted his hand up to touch the brim of the black Stetson in greeting, he was handsome, he had a scar under one eye, a crescent faded white like a little sleeping quarter moon, he had a straight nose and a square chin, the scar was something that he must have gotten as a boy back in Durango, Mariposa thought, he was tall, and the young men with him greeted her politely, she knew they all worked on the same construction site together, and quiet, rather shy Ignacio told her to bring Carta Blancas for all of them, he was paying, a cold Carta Blanca for him and one for each of his five *compadres*, anything she wanted for herself, too, though she told him that she didn't need anything, she was fine, and soon Mariposa was coming back with the order through the bar area, where the crowd was thinning out now and where Mariposa concentrated on not bumping into anybody, looking at the six wobbly bottles on the tray she held in front of her, it was heavy with the many Carta Blancas and she had to be especially careful, they jangled against each other as she walked in the beige sandals, Mariposa very, very serious in balancing the tray before her as she moved along, then smiling with obvious relief when she finally set the tray on a chair next to the men sitting there, she wrapped the bottles one by one, she carefully encased each in a little white shroud of a napkin, passed a bottle to each of the men, she left her tray on the chair and then sat on another empty metal folding chair right next to Ignacio, the place that was, of course, waiting for her, Ignacio told her she should keep a running tab, she told him she knew that, and she also knew, though she didn't tell him, that he would eventually talk a little about his favorite *fútbol* team, Chivas from Guadalajara, and she also knew that he would talk about the other men, never himself, quietly,

he was head of their Mexican crew on the job, a
foreman, and the week before he had told a story about
Armando now sitting there, Ignacio smilingly and
quietly had told how sturdy Armando, with his black
hair cut in a true brush so it stood straight up on his
bull's head, Armando had left a big slab of plywood with
the end of it hanging over an open, uncompleted
stairwell, a shaft without the stairs installed yet and
three stories up, the plywood was to be nailed there as
floor decking before it would be cut along the edge of
the stairwell that it was overhanging by a foot or so, he
would lob off the excess so it would fit along the
stairwell opening, Armando went off to get a power saw
for the cut, a Skilsaw, and Ignacio had told Mariposa
that a power saw was called in English exactly that, a
Skilsaw, it had all happened on that very high third story
of the condominium complex they were working on,
and, sure enough, Armando came back with the saw,
spreading his feet in work boots to get a good stance for
when he leaned over to make the straight cut with the
saw's whirring blade and forgetting that he hadn't
already nailed down the sheet of knotty plywood yet,
Armando stepped flat onto the overhanging part, so that
the whole sheet flipped out under his weight, Armando
riding the plywood down the full three stories of the

stairwell, Mariposa had pictured him on maybe a
magically flying surfboard, there were minor scrapes and
bruises from banging along the concrete walls of the
shaft of the hollow stairwell, but he was OK, near
miraculously, and the head boss on the site, the Anglo
patrón, had witnessed the whole episode, telling
Armando that he would give him time and a half on the
hourly wage for the specific hour in which the accident
had happened, the boss had called it in English "flight
pay," and that meant what is called in Spanish *la paga de
vuelo,* Ignacio had explained to Mariposa, Ignacio liking
the joke of the words the boss had used, he said,
because Armando had been *flying*, all right, the others
smiling, liking the story Ignacio had told, too, they all
liked Ignacio, she knew, he was the foreman of their
crew, it had been a funny story, and sturdy, dark-
complexioned Armando with his bull's head and that
brush-cut pomaded straight up for going out like this on
a Saturday night had seemed, in a way, very proud that
handsome Ignacio had told a story about him, but that
had been the Saturday before, and Mariposa asked
Armando about it now, Mariposa sitting beside Ignacio
who smelled of his minty aftershave, who smelled
somehow very *clean*, she asked Armando if he had
received any more *paga de vuelo* since she had last seen

him the Saturday before, and Armando smiled, the others smiled, even laughed, and sitting there Mariposa listened to the music, watched the dancing along with the others, none of them ever danced, they liked to just watch on Saturday night, the music was blaringly loud, as usual, and here by the dance floor the smoke was thick and reddish in the light, but Mariposa was feeling much better, happy even, very happy, and when she crossed her legs at the knee she felt the ballpoint pen in the jeans' front pocket, poking her and uncomfortable there, the orange-and-white thing advertising a U-Haul franchise, and from under the brim of the dressy Stetson mustached Ignacio looked straight ahead, kept watching the dancing, Mariposa uncrossed her legs, then extended them, raised her behind up a bit in the chair, to take the pen out of the tight front pocket and put it into the embroidered back pocket, the two white plastic bracelets clicking together on her wrist, she had no watch, but before slipping the pen into the back pocket she remembered the napkin she had placed in the other back pocket, and reaching around with the other hand she lifted it out, unfolded it, and looked at it again, BILL, RODEWAY INN, I-35, ROOM 224, Mariposa smiling, she would call him tomorrow, definitely, she thought how lucky she was to have met him, and then

Ignacio looked over to ask her what she had there, she told him it was something that had to do with work she was looking into, *empleo, trabajo,* and Ignacio nodded, seemingly approving, seemingly liking the sensibleness of it, and Mariposa liked the idea that Ignacio saw her as somebody sensible and practical, a girl looking for better work, Ignacio surely understood her situation, and she wanted to think that he knew that she, Mariposa, shouldn't be working as a B-girl, a taxi-dancer, it was only temporary, Mariposa would find other work, of course, and Mariposa carefully folded the napkin again, she leaned forward to tuck it into the pocket of the jeans, then she slid the pen into that pocket, too, she relaxed and let her back, bare in the lime-green halter top, ease against the chair, and looking straight ahead again and not at her, Ignacio slowly did what he had done on other Saturday nights, quietly, very gentlemanly, he raised his arm and slowly put it over the back of her chair, onto her shoulders, Mariposa liked that, his shirt had roses thickly embroidered on the front, a cluster of them on either side of the buttons on the shirt's sheened black cloth, blossoming red roses with abundant green leaves, and the Saturday before as they sat there together he had even bought her a single long-stemmed rose, one from a vendor who had come in on his rounds, and maybe Ignacio would do it again this Saturday night if the vendor who had already been in once did show up again, she sat there like that with Ignacio's arm comfortably over her shoulders, they watched the dancing together, the other young men sitting with them on folding chairs there at the side of the dance floor watched the dancing, Mariposa felt very happy, La canción de Mariposa, and she was Mariposa, she was Mariposa who had been in Nuevo Laredo and Tennessee and now, very definitely, Austin, Texas, she was from Honduras and not Mexico, which made her different, and it was getting quite late at the Club El Pájaro Verde, and . . .

About the Author

Peter LaSalle is the author of several books of fiction, including the novel *Strange Sunlight* and, most recently, a story collection, *Tell Borges If You See Him*. His work has appeared in magazines and anthologies such as *Tin House, Zoetrope, Paris Review, Best American Short Stories, Best American Mystery Stories, Sports Best Short Stories,* and *Prize Stories: The O. Henry Awards*. He has taught at universities in this country and in France, and in 2005 received the Award for Distinguished Prose from the *Antioch Review*. He lives in Austin, Texas.